To Claire
and your child within!

With admiration
        Leonora   30/04/12

LET THE CHILDREN SING

LET THE CHILDREN SING

Leonora Langley

The Book Guild Ltd
Sussex, England

First published in Great Britain in 2004 by
The Book Guild Ltd
25 High Street
Lewes, East Sussex
BN7 2LU

Typesetting in Times by
Keyboard Services, Luton, Bedfordshire

Printed in Great Britain by
CPI Bath

A catalogue record for this book is available from
The British Library

ISBN 1 85776 872 8

*This book is dedicated to my Mother,
Robert, Felicity and Charlie – all
amazingly inspirational*

Contents

PART ONE

PART TWO

A compilation of exclusive interviews with children's services, children, parents, teachers, classroom assistants, headteachers, university professors, educationists, educational psychologists and psychotherapists on how we might better enable young people to gain more fulfilment and enjoyment from their home lives and school environments in relation to greater awareness of emotional development and the nurturing of feelings.

'The School Boy'

(Songs of Innocence and of Experience)

by William Blake

I love to rise in a summer morn,
When the birds sing on every tree;
The distant huntsman winds his horn,
And the sky-lark sings with me.
O! what sweet company.

But to go to school in a summer morn
O! it drives all joy away;
Under a cruel eye outworn,
The little ones spend their day,
In sighing and dismay.

Ah! then at times I drooping sit,
And spend many an anxious hour.
Nor in my book can I take delight,
Nor sit in learning's bower,
Worn thro' with the dreary shower.

How can the bird that is born for joy,
Sit in a cage and sing.
How can a child when fears annoy,

But droop his tender wing,
And forget his youthful spring.

O! father and mother, if buds are nip'd,
And blossoms blown away,
And if the tender plants are strip'd
Of their joy in the springing day,
By sorrow and care's dismay,

How shall the summer arise in joy
Or the summer fruits appear,
Or how shall we gather what griefs destroy
Or bless the mellowing year,
When the blasts of winter appear.

PART ONE

Introduction

It was harvest festival, and my six-year-old son's angelic singing voice rang through the school hall. I tried to make eye contact to let him know his efforts weren't in vain, but he was completely masked by a group of children at least a head taller than him. As the children sat down and my eyes finally met his, tears were rolling down his face. I swallowed hard as I recalled another six-year-old with a lovely voice, masked by another group of children, on another special occasion, on another school stage forty years ago. It was hard to believe that my child could be experiencing exactly the same frustration and despair in 1997 as I had back in 1957. But he, too, was part of an institution where the individual spirit is crushed and moulded into a collective consciousness of conformity.

Throughout the history of education, which formally began in Britain in the 1870s with the introduction of compulsory schooling for the masses, there has been an ongoing debate as to whether education is an individual or societal process. Most people believe that it cannot be one without the other because if a person cannot read or write they are of little use to society or themselves. Whatever its practical aims, ideally, education should inspire and transform individuals as well as society as a whole. In reality, it is, for the most part, uninspiring and stagnant.

I am convinced that the fundamental problem with

3

mainstream schooling in the UK, and the state education system of several other countries, is its emphasis on the functional and mechanical, which produces automatons, or else fragmented human beings with deep psychological problems, unable to cope with the real and diverse challenges of life. Since the late 1980s, when the UK government took interventionist measures to regulate education, most notably with the introduction of the National Curriculum, this problem has become increasingly apparent.

The schools of today may be better funded, better staffed and better equipped, but it is only by de-emphasising the quantifying notion of teaching, which is based on the acquisition and memorisation of facts and figures, that we are ever going to help young people to become better-balanced and more fulfilled human beings. We teach children to divide things and examine separate parts instead of encouraging them to look at the whole picture. We offer them a narrow, mechanical and material view of life but provide limited access to the magic and fantasy of childhood. We focus on cognitive skills and logical reasoning and offer few opportunities for emotional responses.

But it is not enough for children to be imbued with outer and visible things. They also need inner and invisible nourishment. We need to place more emphasis on children's immaterial needs and bring creativity, which deals with the emotive and imaginative aspects of their psyches, into the main frame of the curriculum. As it stands, our education system not only limits children's emotional development, it seems to encourage young people to be at odds with each other rather than at one. A rich emotional language can help children process decisions as well as nurture self-awareness, motivation, empathy and hope, while a restricted emotional language renders them handicapped and isolated.

The salient question we need to ask is what are we educating for? Is it simply for basic survival and a vocational

4

means-to-an-end, or is it for enriching existence and engendering the joy of living? It is predicted that many of us will be working a three-day week within the next decade, and there will be more opportunities to work from home. This will lead to increased leisure time and the opportunity to explore life in a more holistic way. We need to prepare for a time when there will be less emphasis on the vocational and more on enriching the quality of our personal lives. For this to happen, children's education has to be structured not only to fulfil the nature of society's needs in terms of production skills for its workforce, but also to reflect the nature of the children themselves. It makes sense to create an environment in the home and at school which is more responsive to children's natures.

We need to pay greater heed to the naturalists' interpretation of the word 'education', derived from the Latin *educere*, meaning to lead out, rather than the formalists' interpretation of *educare* which means to 'form' or 'train'. Today, more than ever, we seem to be forcing in, cramming overburdened young minds with ever more knowledge so as to become competent, if miserable, computer-like databases. But the more we model ourselves after machines or computers, which rely on quantities and measures, the more we depersonalise and devalue our lives and environment. If we take heed of Dostoevsky's belief that his own intellectual capacity represented only one-twentieth of his whole capacity, then schools are certainly on a lopsided mission by failing to develop and nurture all aspects of children's complex natures.

By concentrating on a small part of a child's potential and making it the whole, we are ignoring the possibility of fostering completely integrated individuals – thinking beings, but also feeling and dreaming beings.

I believe the fundamental purpose of our existence on this planet is to create. Human beings are not only *Homo sapiens* but also *Homo aestheticus*. It is our creative capacity which sets us apart from other living forms, and anything that stifles that basic impulse within us is destructive. While we need the left-brain facility of logical and scientific reasoning, it is the nurturing of our artistic right side of the brain, our inward state of being, that brings us most joy and fulfilment. The left and right hemispheres of the brain need to work in integrated harmony. It's time to bring head and heart into the classroom as equal partners. Even the sciences need to be 'felt' and have their origins in creative experiences. Children need to be aesthetically, as well as intellectually, moved by the wonder and mystery of nature.

There are many teachers with artistic sensibilities who strive for the humanistic and nurturing approach to teaching, but, however creative and courageous they may be, there is little scope to embrace the sentient and imaginative aspects of children's personalities within the bread-and-butter constraints imposed by the present emphasis of the National Curriculum. As empirical test results improve, the condition of the human spirit and its aesthetic sensibility seems to become even more stifled. But we can restrain and control for only so long without rebellion.

Inevitable backlashes against the mechanical and objective doctrines firmly rooted in our schools are manifest in the growing drug culture, the rise in teenage pregnancies, rave discos, football hooliganism, an addiction to computers, the Internet and television, and, for children, an obsession with trading card games which can become so consuming that there is no space in their heads for anything else. Whatever form of escape people turn to, it represents a numbing and desensitising reaction against the authoritarian nature of our education system. In a sense, the automatons of our schools are destined to become the automatons of our society.

Greater emphasis on scientific and logical thinking, made possible by technological innovation, has certainly brought greater financial prosperity to our Western culture. As organised religion declines and the ringing of church bells gives way to the ringing of checkout tills, there is no denying that we live in an increasingly materialistic world. But greater outer benefits have brought deeper inward deficits to the human psyche, with the subsequent dehumanising effect on individuals. The pursuit of spiritual sustenance and qualities such as kindness and compassion have become less desirable than the pursuit of fame and fortune. The majority of children have an absolute belief that becoming a movie actor or football star is the pinnacle of achievement, a view that is often shared by their parents, the media and society.

While young people enjoy certain elements of the material benefits of modern life, they cannot fail to wonder about a higher spiritual purpose. They seem to have an innate need to be bonded to something divine or spiritual, providing a sense of unity and belonging. They look to sensitive teachers to help them understand what they are doing here and how to make the most of their brief time on this planet. They sense that there is more to education than learning how to parrot facts and perform as mechanical processors in a system that places so much emphasis on academic achievement.

It's time to help young people explore the possibilities of education as a liberating process, an opening up and broadening of the mind, where aesthetic, spiritual, moral and physical issues are given the same consideration as functional processes. At the moment, too much credence is given to conveying knowledge rather than exploring it through feelings and emotions. What children feel is just as important as what they think. The more we can access children's feeling centres, the more evident it becomes that what we teach the young goes far beyond the confines of what they learn in schools. It's a lifelong process of creating integrated, free-thinking human beings able to explore the meaning of life in an intelligent and creative way.

As our Western culture zips along at a frenetic pace, many young people must be left gasping for breath. Children are told to 'hurry up' and 'come on' at least fifty times a day. All this hurrying, administered by impatient adults, encourages children to rush at everything, including their food, their play, their school work, their very life. Many must feel that 'Hurryup' is their given name. Such pressure creates tense and stressed-out children who are finally rendered incapable of maintaining such a breakneck schedule. It is hardly surprising that they finally rebel and refuse to cooperate at all.

Often marginalised by the mainstream culture of education, today's youth is convinced that many of the problems in school are caused by the problems with school. Students complain that much of the school day is a waste of time and completely unrelated to their lives. They express feelings of isolation, detachment and alienation from their teachers and peers. They speak of too much control from teachers and the need to have a greater say in how and what they learn. They feel undervalued as individuals, overwhelmed by competition and stress and are tired of being judged purely on exam results. They are looking for that elusive something that they cannot name, something that will make them feel whole, or at least less fragmented.

I've spoken to many young people who are yearning for education that is more personal and human. They want a learning experience that places more emphasis on what will help them to make sense of their lives and the world around them. They already have access to all the facts and figures they need via computers and the Internet. What they search for is meaning in the mountain of facts and information that they are given in a bid to make them better human beings. Above all, they seek personal development and self-acceptance as well as an appreciation and acceptance of others.

For any of this to happen, the teaching/learning model for the future needs to fully embrace every individual as a feeling and emotional person with a free will to create. It all comes down to educators balancing the subject content with the pupils' feelings, emotions and personal experiences. A starting point would be to introduce more humanistic strategies into the curriculum which, I believe, can most powerfully and holistically be done through greater emphasis on the arts.

Human beings have complex natures but it is becoming increasingly apparent that the artistic esoteric side, rather than the logical, is closer to our intrinsic structure. By empowering children to become creators of literature, music, dance, art, drama and film, they begin to get in touch with the individuality of their unique essence. When individual consciousness is nurtured, a common symbolic purpose starts to emerge which leads to a broader cultural and global awareness as well as a greater sense of unity for future generations.

It may seem like a daunting task to reverse a centuries-old system, based on conformity and technical processing, and transform it into a new and innovative model of creativity and uniqueness, where rigour and imagination go hand in hand. But it is only by merging the scientific and artistic into an organic whole, balancing the yin and the yang, where teachers expand their humanistic and artistic energies, that education is ever going to progress. By studying facts and acquiring mechanical explanations, it may be possible for students to understand the intricacies of a machine but it does not prepare them for life.

It is important to stop regarding poetry, art, music, dance, drama and film as the trimmings of a meat and potatoes diet and start seeing them as vital ingredients in a well-balanced wholesome meal. The arts are no fringe event, they deserve double billing with their scientific counterparts.

The arts not only help to educate the feelings and develop the emotions, they also nurture a capacity for creative thoughts as well as social and moral values. Being free of utilitarian symbols, they help us to get in touch with our souls. It's time to celebrate the feeling, aesthetic and imaginative aspects of children's personalities as well as the thinking and analytical ones, so that they can all come to know, love, value and celebrate their unique role as a wonderful and mystical part of nature and the universe.

Chapter One

The Pre-School Years

Parents as educators

If education is perceived in its broadest sense as a lifelong pursuit, then pre-school experience is at its very roots. The vital role of parents and guardians as educators of the young cannot be overestimated in developing sound emotional stability, especially in the first few years. Parents are children's foremost teachers for the pre-school years and co-teachers for the duration of their education.

A generation ago, when men were the main breadwinners and women were confined to the house and nursery as homemakers, most parents were so preoccupied with economic survival that physical needs took precedence over emotional development. It was sufficient to feed, clothe and keep a roof over children's heads. While there are still many children who never acquire the most basic of building blocks and are victims of the perpetuation of the intimidation and indoctrination which have been handed down from generation to generation, often living under constant economic and social stress with parents who can barely skim the surface of their own emotional wounds let alone their children's, there are many young people who now have the opportunity to lead fulfilled lives.

For the first time in our history, children have the possibility to experience both the milk and honey of life, not least

11

because until the twentieth century two-thirds of children died in childhood. Witnessing a dramatic decrease in infant mortality and the birth of a number of new child welfare organisations, the twentieth century became known as 'The Century of the Child'. Within the framework of a more stable economy, the back-up of the welfare state and the opportunity for women to contribute in the workplace, more parents are now able to afford the 'luxury' of considering their children's psychological and emotional well-being and, indeed, their own!

But on entering a new millennium, we still have a long way to go to fulfil all our children's needs. One of the greatest unresolved issues is the daily struggle that parents face between an idealistic notion of how they would like to act towards their children and the reality of how they do act.

We are often reluctant to accept responsibility for any negative effect on our children's development and we have a tendency to blame others for anything that goes wrong – a partner, a teacher, the media, our children's peers and even the children themselves. This is because most parents do not have a conscious desire to harm their children and would be unable to live with the overwhelming guilt of owning up to such a 'crime'. But the truth is that all parents, however unwittingly, inflict a great deal of pain and shame on their offspring. Some children are so badly treated that they must wonder why they were conceived in the first place. It can be particularly confusing for children, as most of the maltreatment is administered in the name of love (or under the guise of love).

Motives for procreation

I've always felt that if women needed a licence to have a child, it might make us think twice about our motives for wanting a baby and the commitment and responsibility that goes with motherhood. Other than an innate biological need, there can be more strategic factors at play in the reproductive equation. Some women feel obliged to procreate either to please a partner or their parents, to have someone in their image or to have a companion in old age. Some even regard their offspring like a trophy, another material possession that might elevate their self-worth, look good on their biography or serve as a toy or plaything that can be picked up or discarded at will. We have to face the truth that many children are created as mere tokens of repressed needs and given little respect by their parents. Either regarded as a major burden or minor irritation, they're manipulated and controlled into an emotional prison to which the parents hold the key.

Very often, oppression and submission begin in the first weeks of infants' lives as their innocence and dependency are exploited and subjugated into conformity and an expectation of achievement. They're fed seductive words and accept them as received wisdom in the belief that parents know best. What's really sad is that young children will idealise and protect their parents no matter what they do or say to them. Children have an inbuilt tendency to blame themselves for any pain inflicted by the parents. There can be nothing more confusing for children than to be confronted by an antagonist whom they love.

Unconditional love

At the root of a child's repressed experience is invariably a mother who is physically present but emotionally unavailable to engage in a close relationship with a child. She is often not consciously aware of her emotional ineptitude, as this is a legacy from her own repressed childhood that makes her

13

blind to her children's emotional needs. She is simply unable to offer unconditional love. Such a mother might well be prone to excessive post-natal depression or show a resistance to breastfeeding, which is arguably the greatest way to bond with a newborn child. While many mothers feel that it's a child's birthright to be offered breast milk, and that suckling on the breast offers an infant greater security and comfort as well as essential nutrients, some women see it as a physically painful and time-consuming chore.

There are some mothers who admit to experiencing no maternal feelings at all and who are unaware of the totality of attention and love needed to nurture their helpless infant. Some are so desperate to return to work and re-establish their professional identity that they are prepared to place their newborn baby in the care of a perfect stranger. Determined to have a separate existence with the minimum amount of contact and 'interference' from their baby, many professional women will not allow a child to undermine their masterplan for 'having it all'. But what they often fail to realise is that, while they may be finding self-fulfilment, their child will probably end up with very little self-fulfilment indeed. From the cradle to the grave, love is the emotional food that everyone yearns for. If children do not receive maternal love in the early stages of their lives, to feel that they are loved simply because they exist, they will be less likely to find satisfaction in future intimate relationships – including a relationship with themselves.

Arguments for relinquishing the mothering role so early encompass economic necessity, lack of mental stimulation, the pursuit of a more balanced lifestyle, burning ambition and the not uncommon experience of liking children but disliking babies! These are all very real to the mother's sense of loss of identity but so, too, are the feelings of abandonment experienced by their children, feelings they will carry for the rest of their lives.

In weighing up their priorities, many mothers, after experiencing the vicelike grip of their baby's tiny fingers around theirs, would not wish to miss their child's first smile, first footsteps, first words – seminal moments that can never be recaptured.

The fear of motherhood

What often underlies a woman's desire to escape from motherhood is the intrinsic fear it can engender. It can trigger unexpected emotions and feelings of inadequacy, such as anonymity, helplessness and isolation, which were unexpressed in her own childhood. Such emotional responses can be intimidating and embarrassing. Through the eyes of a child, a mother can relive her own humiliating past and feel compelled to retreat to the relative safety of the workplace so that she doesn't have to confront her own demons. But if she had the courage to face 'the agony and the ecstasy' associated with being a mother, it might help her to get in touch with her own emotional wounds, resolve them and prevent them from being handed down to her child.

Motherhood has an uncanny habit of revealing a triangular perspective on human interaction. Firstly, there is the child's view, secondly, there is the view of the child the mother once was and, thirdly, the adult view of the mother she now is. Such perspectives can evoke and provoke all sorts of emotional turmoil which is better resolved than ignored.

A large part of the resolution is being able to recognise that a mother sees a mirror image of herself in her child, be it conscious or unconscious, and does not necessarily like what she sees. A mother is happy when she sees characteristics in her child that she likes in herself but is not so pleased when she sees traits that she dislikes in her own make-up. To prevent herself from offering only a conditioned response to her child, she needs to recall and relive her own conscious and unconscious childhood memories. She can then try to analyse her own behaviour patterns in order to understand how she is influencing and moulding her child's behaviour. Rather than using reason and logic in handling her child, a mother is very often inflicting her own emotional baggage. For every woman who is able to acknowledge her own emotional issues and try to resolve them, there are many more who never come to terms with this painful process and will find an escape route at the first opportunity.

No matter how dedicated a mother might be, the general trend over the past decade amongst the six million mothers in Britain has been to resume part-time work once a child reaches the toddler stage and to find alternative care for their young children. But this is a trend that is slowly changing. While many agencies feed mothers the idea that child-rearing is holding them back from a more fulfilling existence and that nurseries offer the promise of a more stimulating environment for children in the company of their peers, an increasing number of mothers are standing their ground and asking for permission to stay home and do the job themselves. They are realising that, while some children may do better in childcare than they would in the care of their mothers, many will do worse.

Loyalty to children

Mature mothers who have fulfilled themselves in the workplace are more prepared to put a career on hold for the first few years of their infant's life. They are able to accept that by losing their old identity, they could well acquire a new and better one. They are more open to throwing themselves wholeheartedly into the experience in the knowledge that any resentment or half-hearted sham at mothering will be picked up by their children, if not in their childhood then certainly in their adulthood.

In the last quarter century, women have been led to believe that they can have it all. Yes, we can, but not all at the same time. I can remember that caring for my young son filled all the 'brain space' that had once launched and sustained my career. Suddenly, I didn't have the energy, capability or desire to continue on the same professional path. The passion for my career was now transferred to a passion for caring for my son. For the first few years of his life, I felt I had no choice but to put my ambitions for furthering my career firmly on the back burner. It's unrealistic to think that we can simultaneously juggle the responsibilities of motherhood and a full-time career successfully, especially during an infant's exploratory stage – the first eighteen months of life. By putting a career first, something has to give, and it's inevitably the child who gets the thin edge of the wedge.

A woman who makes a conscious decision to become a full-time mother needs to be applauded and fully supported by society. The government's recent proposal to pay a parent up to £150 a week to stay home is commendable. There seems to be no sensible reasoning behind a mother returning to work so that she can earn enough to pay someone else to look after her child. Even a high-earner cannot justify leaving her child, because it's not materialism that a child needs but an available mother who can give unconditional love, or at least try to.

Making the adjustment from career woman to devoted mother is incredibly difficult to start with, but it is possible. There are many stories of women who, once immersed in mothering, actually grow to prefer looking after their babies and cannot understand their former addiction to a career. However convincing employers may be that it's in a mother's

17

best interests to keep working, they are not acting in the best interests of a child. In the early years of a child's life, a father also needs to let his employer know that his family comes first. The realisation that your boss will dismiss you if it suits them tends to put things into perspective. A child cannot be so easily dismissed without painful consequences. Parents' loyalties should not be primarily to their bosses but to their children.

Very often, a first-time mother has an overwhelming feeling that her life will never return to normal. But it does. Everything is cyclical and children's needs don't remain the same forever. Above all, we need to be flexible and allow our children to guide us through. When infants urge us to leave the housework and go to the park, they are simply telling us it's time to convene with nature. In many cases, baby knows best.

It may be a cliché, but it's important to bear in mind that childhood is fleeting. A parent and child only get one shot at it. So many children are robbed of an authentic childhood by egocentric mothers straining at the bit to keep proving themselves in the workplace or resume a carefree life. But motherhood can also be carefree. Like everything else, it all depends on how we approach it and how much we're prepared to give. Being a parent is by far the most important and challenging job we can have and it doesn't come with a manual.

It's hardly surprising that parents invariably speak of their firstborn being the subject of experimentation and of feeling more confident and relaxed with a second child. Since parenting is a creative art and not a science, or a subject taught in schools, there is no tried-and-tested formula for getting it right. It all comes down to a highly refined instinct and the capacity to give unconditional love.

Emotional stability

The greatest gift parents can bestow upon their children is sound emotional health, to allow them the opportunity to get in touch with their feeling centre. It's an essential building block, through which children learn to structure their lives, and is the key to all other aspects of their future development. Emotions play an integral role in nurturing thought processes, self-perception, persistence and social aptitude. Unfortunately, children's emotional nurturing is invariably a haphazard and unimaginative process built on shaky foundations, rendering them incapable of fulfilling their true potential.

Without access to their true emotions and 'real selves', children will always experience difficulty in making sound judgements and forever remain in a repressed, childish state. If they disown their feelings, especially the negative emotions of anger, frustration, fear and sadness (all of which help children connect with their inner truths), they will later project them onto others and become unintegrated people who are doomed to a life of emotional deprivation. Children who are deprived of a full range of feelings will not have access to their souls. The awful truth is that the Western world operates on the premise that being rational and reasonable is preferable to being emotional. But there's nothing more powerful than vulnerability.

The overpowering effect of negative emotions, particularly anger and frustration, can have a terrifying effect on children when they first confront them. Instead of receiving reassurance when they get angry and frustrated, children are often confronted with more anger and frustration from their parents. This acts like an incendiary device which fuels both parties. To protect themselves from such a negative confrontation, children keep yelling and screaming and forcing their parents to give in to their outbursts. This encourages children to

19

repeat the performance on future occasions just to get their own way.

Such negative outcomes might have been prevented had the parents acted less capriciously. Children tend to learn more about anger from parents who are moderately expressive, rather than overreactive or whimsical, both opposite ends of the emotional spectrum. Distressed children need to be held and comforted, to be shown that their parents are in complete control of their own emotions. They can then begin to learn that negative emotions can be dealt with in a positive way and reassured that, even when they are expressing anger, they are still cherished. Unless children are allowed to fully express their negative emotions, come to terms with them and then learn to calm down and resume a state of equilibrium, they will grow up to be terrified every time they begin to experience them.

Nurturing a calm child

A vital part of parenting is teaching children basic emotional competence in handling their frustrations and controlling their emotions so that they can cope with whatever life throws at them. While physical activity can do a great deal to release children's anger and frustration, it is the patient and reassuring guidance of their parents that children need most in the handling of negative emotions. By nurturing a calm baby, a parent is preparing a child to be more self-reliant and resilient in childhood and beyond. The last thing an angry child needs is an angry parent. Children who are on the receiving end of frequent, uncontrollable emotional outbursts from a parent can regard the expression of emotions as a danger zone. They tend to clam up and stop expressing their own emotions because they associate their expression with another 'dramatic scene'. In a family where one parent tends to be more overreactive than the other, the children are more likely to build up a stronger emotional tie with the less volatile parent because they trust their response to be more rational.

There is no doubt that having children puts us in touch with our most uncontrolled impulses. This is especially true in a high-arousal situation such as a breakage or a spillage. An overreactive parent can be easily provoked when a child has an accident around the house. If a parent had the capacity to look beyond the material damage or loss and see the incident from the child's vantage point, they would see a young person with terror in their eyes, someone who feels shamed by their inadequacy and is fearful of parental anger.

Adults need to recognise that it is often their lack of forethought that contributes to accidents. A precious vase or uncorked bottle of wine could well have been left within easy reach of the child, and damage to an expensive carpet is hardly comparable to the damage of a child's priceless sense of self.

A child's emotional response to an accident like this is rarely considered, because most adults were not given the emotional resources to deal with similar situations themselves when they were children. Many adults may be acting 'in their adult' for a good deal of the time, but at the slightest provocation they can easily revert to being 'a three-year-old' and re-enact the emotional turmoil of infancy. When they do this, they tend to exaggerate the gravity of a child's temper tantrums and overreact to them.

Protecting the unborn

Those of us who had our emotional needs met, a fortunate minority, will be better able to nurture emotional stability in their children. They will be more aware that from the moment a child is conceived, they are able to pick up on their parents' joy or disappointment about the pregnancy. A foetus is capable of a range of emotions and sensual experiences, such as seeing, tasting, hearing and, most importantly, feeling, which is why it is vital for a child to feel wanted and accepted in its embryonic state. Scientists have proven that a foetus has a short-term memory of at least ten minutes and a long-term memory of at least a day. Recent research has also shown that the developing foetus is able to respond to music, lullabies in particular. The unborn child can move to the rhythm of its mother's voice and seems to develop more quickly outside the womb when exposed to classical music for ten minutes a day.

Everything the mother experiences whilst she is carrying her baby affects the unborn child in some way. In particular, the relationship between a mother and her partner can have a profound effect on an unborn child. A loving and mutually respectful relationship is obviously preferable to a stormy, unsettled one and is likely to help predetermine a child's future emotional well-being. The mood of the expectant mother is also known to influence a baby's development. Babies of depressed mothers are more likely to become depressed children. Of vital importance to the physical health of the baby is a mother's choice of foods and nutritional supplements, before and during the pregnancy, and the avoidance of chemical substances. The toxins produced by a mother who smokes, takes drugs or consumes alcohol whilst pregnant can inflict untold physical distress and emotional trauma on a growing baby.

The birthing process

When a baby finally reaches maturation and prepares to leave the security and comfort of the womb, its passage to the outside world needs to be as serene and stress-free as possible. Being born is arguably the most stressful event of a human being's life. Not only does the foetus endure physical and emotional trauma in coming down the birth canal in preparation for its first breath, it also assimilates the emotional state of its mother at the time of birth. Any uncertainty and misgivings from the mother can create all sorts of complications. At this time, a mother needs to communicate to her child that the world lights up with endless possibilities.

On drawing their first breath and uttering their first cry, babies have to adapt to life outside the womb within a matter of seconds. They have to assimilate to a dry world after coming from a wet environment, adapt to a lower temperature, start breathing their own oxygen, and switch from a world of muffled sounds to a world of distinct sounds which include their own piercing cry. As soon as my son was born, I remember feeling overawed as I watched his head turning and his eyes making rapid movements in response to the various voices in the delivery room.

Babies' first impressions of life are vitally important and yet their first experiences are likely to be filled with trauma, pain and abandonment. It never felt right that my son was whisked away from me to be weighed, measured and tested so soon after his birth. Although he was later returned for his first feed, which was entirely masterminded by him as he 'latched on' with the greatest of ease, he was soon taken away again to spend the night in a baby unit. I was assured that I needed a good night's sleep, but my thoughts were only for him as he lay, probably weeping, in the confines of a small crib, unable to make human contact, partially sighted and hearing only the cries of other needy babies. In my ignorant and dazed state, I went along with it all, believing that the medical profession knew best. In retrospect, there is nobody more knowing than a loving mother and her instinctual response to her child's needs.

A cry for help

When babies leave hospital, they are now at the mercy of their mothers in all sorts of new ways. They have an instinctual desire to make contact with the warmth and texture of human skin, to hear the tender response of a human voice and the reassuring heartbeat of their mother, to suckle on the breast. Their need to be held in their mother's arms is absolutely vital to their well-being. Babies love being soothed by a lullaby, and enjoy the nonsense sounds – the gurgling and gooing and grimacing – of communicating with their parents. And yet we tend to physically isolate, even banish, them to the nursery for long periods of the day and night, ignoring their cries for help.

The way a mother responds to her baby's crying often depends on how she was treated as a baby. If a mother's crying was ignored when she was young, she is more likely to have a similar response to her baby. But a mother needs to understand that babies don't cry for nothing. They are communicating in the only way they know how, and their pleas for help need to be taken seriously. They are either wet, hungry, tired, unwell or in need of emotional comfort. A reassuring cuddle is often all they need. Existence is often overwhelmingly scary for adults. Babies, who have fewer resources, need much reassurance from a source other than themselves.

And yet the measures some parents will resort to to ensure a good night's sleep – usually those who are desperate to maintain a professional life – are quite horrifying. I knew a couple who employed a specialist live-in nanny for the first month of their son's life to 'train' him to sleep through the night so that they could continue their demanding careers. The essential ingredient of the regime was to ignore the baby's cry until the morning. I knew another mother who did exactly the same thing without the aid of a nanny but with the coercion of her husband. Today she is haunted by the memory of such neglect and has bouts of inconsolable weeping at the thought of having allowed her now ex-husband to influence her in such a way.

A mother needs to accept that a certain amount of sleep deprivation and feeding-on-demand are part and parcel of the mothering process. If a mother is not 'fit to work' the next day, it's because mother nature is urging her to stay at home with the baby.

No matter how many baby books advise a mother seeking a good night's sleep to ignore the cry of her baby, I think they are ill-advised. Of course, a baby can be conditioned to do almost anything you want it to, including sleeping through the night. After crying for prolonged periods and getting no response from their mother, a baby will eventually fall asleep from sheer physical exhaustion, but a sense of betrayal and mistrust will always linger within the child's psyche. It is well documented that there is a strong link between people with psychosexual problems and those adults whose crying as babies was ignored.

Once a mother's instinctual response, which can become almost telepathic, is sufficiently attuned to her baby's needs, bouts of crying can be considerably reduced, if not eliminated. If babies' needs are fully met, they become secure in the knowledge that they are safe and have no need to cry. Sadly, there are not enough infants who experience such contentment. There are far too many babies whose constant crying can tip a parent or childminder over the edge and lead them to shake a helpless infant like a rag doll. We now know that this can do untold cerebral damage and can even lead to death.

One such fatality was described at Leeds Crown Court in November 2000 after a 6-month-old baby boy was left alone for just 15 minutes with a 23-year-old man, the boyfriend of the baby's mother. In the absence of the 18-year-old mother, who was working, and the baby's grandmother, who had gone to collect a prescription for her grandson, the man had been engrossed in a computer game and lost his temper when disturbed by the baby's incessant crying. He shook the baby so violently that he caused a massive blood clot in the infant's brain. The man, who was not the baby's father, was jailed for just three years after admitting manslaughter.

The role of the father

Although we live in a society which tends to marginalise the role of the father, it is still very important in the upbringing of a child. A boy needs a father, or at least a good male role model, to learn how to be a man and a girl needs a father, or a good role model, to learn how to choose a man. In many cases, the expectation that men should be breadwinners has often distanced them from their children. Many feel excluded by the mother/child bonding experience, especially in the first year of a baby's life.

Not only are they unable to carry the baby in their bodies, they are also unable to feed and sustain it. A man can feel jealous and insecure when the mother gives her newborn the undivided attention it needs. A sensitive mother will try to ensure that the father is allowed every opportunity to hold, change, bathe and play with the infant. This will help to nurture the feminine side of the father's nature, which will not only benefit the baby and make the man a better parent but also consolidate the relationship between mother and father and secure a happier long-term future for the child.

Parental expectations

It may seem like an unrealistic expectation within the context of the modern world, but newborn infants need to be given a sense of continuity and predictability based on love and respect from both parents. They also need to be taken seriously by parents who are emotionally available as they make an effortless transition from symbiosis to individuation. Above all, children need to feel they're living their own lives and not what's projected on them by their parents. So often children are used as an emotional crutch to bear the sorrow and emptiness of their parents' sense of futility through their own lives. But it is not the duty of children to mend their parents. It will serve no other purpose than to arrest the child's own emotional development and might lead to a crippling, unhealthy enmeshment which could take years of therapy to unravel. Children need to be loved for exactly who they are and not for what they can achieve. After all, children are human beings and not human doings. They need to be reassured that they're loved when they're not doing anything at all.

It is also important that children feel they're getting enough attention. Some children complain that they only get attention when they are sick or doing something that makes their parents proud. But children only have to satisfy their own needs to succeed and do not have to fulfil any expectation or goal set by their parents. Overly high expectations of creating 'perfect children' are often projections of parents' unfulfilled ambitions and can lead children to believe that their parents are more concerned with their performance than with them as people.

Just as children cannot hope for perfect parents, children cannot be moulded to fit their parents' criteria for perfect children. Parents are merely guides to help children develop into the people they wish to become and not what they

27

want them to be. In the same way, parents are not responsible for their children's happiness. No one can expect children to be happy all the time. As long as they have the resources to be able to handle and work through their emotions, children hold the key to their own happiness.

Children need to know that they don't have to act in a certain way to get approval. They must have the opportunity to express a wide range of emotions and moods without having to respond to or accommodate someone else's emotions or moods. This works both ways. But while children need to see parents expressing a range of emotions, it is important that adults do not take their emotions out on their children. Parents need to differentiate between expressing an assertive anger which allows children to feel blameless and a 'dumping' type of anger where children feel responsible for their parents' distress. It's a matter of abandoning aggressive behaviour in favour of stating a need while still respecting the child. By doing this, equality is maintained.

The balance of power

One of the most important aspects of the child–parent relationship is the balance of power. While parents need to teach children clear boundaries in all aspects of life, a point needs to be found where parents and children can meet and function as equals and co-creators in the childhood experience. After all, adults are large children and children small adults. While a child's maturity, general knowledge and life experience are not comparable to an adult's, it is important that parent and child meet on equal terms in regard to their feelings, which transcend age. When responding to a child's emotions, particularly unhappy ones such as anger and sorrow, a parent often treats the child's feelings as small and underdeveloped because the child's physical stature is small and underdeveloped. But children have exactly the same capacity for deep emotional response as adults and their feelings need to be taken very seriously.

As Dr John Collee wrote in the *Observer* in 1990, 'Most children of ten have the mental capacity of adults but, on the crude basis of size and weight, we still deny them access to the adult world. As a result, their behaviour and outlook remains childish and this conveniently provides us with the excuse to discriminate against them. We persist with this because, I suppose, we feel threatened.'

Such discrimination leaves many children unable to express what is going on deep within their unconscious psyches, which means parents have to try and interpret what they are feeling by observing their words and actions. While parents only have what's manifesting on the outside by which to imagine what's going on inside, they have a pretty good idea when they make an effort to put themselves back to the same age as their children are now. It is a question of empathising and respecting children at the particular stage of development they have reached.

All parents are prone to hypervigilance, but, if we could learn to trust and be more relaxed in the company of children by leaving them to their own devices a bit more, everyone would benefit. By their very natures, children are interested in self-preservation and want to do the right thing. An adult's intervention can sometimes place undue pressure on the child and result in their underachievement. Learning to let go is a hard lesson for parents.

Instead of building a relationship which is based on mutual respect, some parents cannot function unless they're in the driving seat. By using their supposed physical and mental superiority, their aim is to break their child's will. This compunction to intimidate their weaker offspring is second nature because that's how they were treated as children. They fail to see that by trying to break a child's will, they are more likely to create an individual who is both wilful and resentful. Children need to know that what is being asked of them comes from a position of love and not a desire to control.

Many parents believe that control is synonymous with discipline. But discipline has nothing to do with control or punishment. The fundamental aim of discipline is to make children self-disciplined. Just as real education is self-education, real discipline is self-discipline. The best way to effect good discipline is to reward children for the things they do well and ignore the things they find difficult. If parents ignore children when they do something well but scream at them for poor behaviour, they are more likely to act badly simply to get attention. Children need to grow in the knowledge that praise is the best form of discipline and punishment the worst. They need to be disciplined by following the example of their parents. A good role model is always preferable to a critic. Parents also need a flexible approach to discipline so that their children are allowed to be themselves. This philosophy can be a threat to parents who think they have to exert extreme measures to get the best out of their children.

Becoming a reasonable parent

So many of us use sweeping statements and gross generalisations when disciplining our children. Some of us even resort to blackmail, either emotional, e.g. 'If you don't stop that, I'll have a stroke!' or material, e.g. 'If you stop kicking your sister, I'll buy you a new pair of trainers!' In fact, a moderate and reasonable parent who does not resort to threats or treats when disciplining a child is likely to get better long-term results.

Parents who are able to offer a balanced explanation as

30

to why a particular mode of behaviour is wrong, and convey to their child that, while their behaviour may be in question, they, as an individual, are intrinsically good, will gain much more respect. Children like parents to discuss what is inappropriate about a particular transgression rather than being told that something is wrong, 'Because I say so!' Children's points of view need to be given full credence. Their opinions and suggestions need to be taken seriously and not dismissed out of hand. Parents can then weigh up their children's desired goals and discuss various options. In this climate of compromise, children will be more willing to modify their behaviour.

Children also need consistency from their parents. They need to know that fair sanctions will be carried out and not just threatened. Without follow-through, parents lose credibility. We need to express our own self-discipline if we are to encourage it in our children. If we do lose our cool, we need to have the courage to admit it and ask a child for forgiveness. It is important for children to know that their parents are capable of saying 'sorry' and to clear the air and start with a clean slate the next day. It is awful for a child to have to go to bed worrying about an unresolved argument with a parent.

Children setting their own values

Criticism and fear, which are both negative forms of punishment, may restrain children from 'doing wrong' in the short term but offer no incentive for 'doing right' in the long term. The only effective form of discipline comes from children's desire to do well in their own eyes and by their own set of values. Good values are nurtured in children by the example of those who care for them. Shouting at children may shock them into obedience or submission but, if they're reasoned with in soft and gentle tones, they will be much more likely to hear what's being said, learn from it and be less likely to repeat it.

While perpetual moaning and intimidation may not occur in every home, the majority of children are subjected to a great deal of verbal put-down. Adults usually have an amazing capacity for self-restraint in their communication with adults such as a spouse, a boss or a friend because they want to be liked and respected by them, yet find it perfectly acceptable to let rip and discharge their anger or frustration on a child. We justify ourselves by saying that children are far too young for harsh words and deeds to have an effect on either their short-term or long-term development. But while children are remarkably resilient and forgiving, they are also a bit like elephants in that they never forget! If we had the opportunity to be a fly on the wall we'd be shocked and shamed by the amount of negativity and gibberish we deliver to our children. It's the same sort of denial that parents who have been feuding for years use when they declare, 'Although we were going through a living hell, it never impacted the kids!'

Children can be very confused when adults, who are meant to be their protectors, suddenly become their detractors. Being nurturers one minute and punishers the next gives young people all sorts of mixed messages and builds up resentment. If children do something which displeases their parents, it is better for them and their parents to be temporarily withdrawn from each other. Sending children to their room provides physical and emotional distance for them to consider their actions and examine their feelings. It is not so much a punishment, more a 'time out' for children and parents to reconsider the situation. Before long, children will invariably be ready to reunite with their parent and come to terms with why the separation was necessary. While temporary separation usually has a positive outcome, a prolonged separation or silence between child and parent invariably causes anxiety and resentment.

Children living in the moment*

It is important to bear in mind that young children have no real concept of past or future time and live entirely in the spontaneity of the moment. They have a limited capability to see how things might impact their future. That is why children who want something right now sometimes have little understanding of needing to wait for it. It is not until we reach middle age that some of us are able to fully understand the meaning of a day or a year within the context of a lifetime.

As children are only aware of what is in their minds right now, parents need to try and work out children's thoughts and their motives with the same immediacy. By letting children know that you have their interests at heart, they are less likely to put up any opposition. Parents can then make suggestions as to how things might be improved. When adults are able to offer the magical combination of emotional empathy while also taking an objective view of the situation, children feel on safe ground for making a compromise.

One of the most difficult things for adults is to know when it is appropriate to restrain and when to allow children to revel in active exploration. Adults easily forget what it's like to be a child with boundless energy and a need for vocal expression, when the world is full of wonder and discovery. So many adults do not like to be in the company of children because they disturb the peace.

They want children to be good and sit still, believing that goodness and immobility are one and the same thing. But since incessant activity is natural in the young, it cannot be right to restrain children's instinctual and natural predisposition to expressing themselves in this way. Similarly, children cannot stop themselves from touching objects in their environment, yet adults are constantly saying, 'Don't touch!' In many instances, children are punished for doing something that is perfectly normal and integral for their sensual and intellectual development.

No kidding kids

Children thrive on honesty. They resent secrets and lies and detest broken promises. No matter how dark or painful the secret, children appreciate the truth. This includes being fully informed of their parents' motives, as in the case of bedtime. Parents who may be in genuine need of a bit of space have to be upfront about why they are sending their children to bed when they're not yet tired. It's not a good idea to tell children that it's in their own interests to get a few extra hours sleep when it's painfully clear to them that it's the parents who want to spend some time alone. Children know when they're tired and they prefer to fall asleep naturally, preferably with a bedtime story. When they are forced to bed by rules and regulations, they will often lie tossing and turning, thinking about why they've been ejected from the comfort of the family unit. If children are to get a good night's sleep, they need to feel wanted and cherished, not neglected and banished.

Adult mentoring

During adolescence, arguments between parents and teenagers are inevitable. As young people struggle for independence against the restriction of curfews, and learn to deal with the temptation of alcohol and drugs which can fill an emotional void, it is normal that they will become more defiant, rebellious and moody. In a state of transition, they certainly don't need parents either to confront or ignore them. More than ever, they need understanding of their problems as they struggle to test limits and find themselves. Trying to impose rules and regulations at this time is probably less appropriate than a flexible and open-minded attitude which will allow them to break free of their parents while still maintaining a close relationship with them. An adult mentor can often assist in the necessary passage of loosening family ties. It can also be helpful for adolescents to be engaged in a passion such as a sport or one of the arts, to help them find an outlet for their considerable energies and frustrations and, hopefully, give greater meaning to their lives.

Smacking children

Although it is hoped that most parents no longer resort to the barbaric use of the rod or belt, smacking is still regarded as a reasonable form of chastisement. In the majority of households, a slap is seen as an immediate quick-fix remedy for a child who is 'acting up', and a good spanking is regarded as an even more effective method of control. Some parents even entrust a childminder with making a judgement about smacking. But surely the odds are heavily stacked against the child? A heavyweight is bound to defeat a featherweight. These are bully-boy tactics in which children have no chance to defend themselves. Such behaviour between adults would be deemed unlawful and, by striking a child, a parent is setting up that child to become a bully.

Children expect adults to be acting in their adult selves and not to be re-enacting their own childhoods as grown-up babies. Counting to ten and exercising a little restraint and a few well-chosen, reasonable words can make life happier for the parent and child. By venting temper and violence on a child, the adult is always the loser. The fact is that smacking a child gets the parent and child nowhere. It is an indication that verbal communication has broken down and been replaced by physical assault. Tragically, these facts are ignored by most parents because they were smacked as children and avow that it did them no harm. But whether they admit it or not, parents who smack regularly can do untold psychological damage to a child, causing long-term mental anguish, fear and intimidation which impact adult relationships.

Taking children's fears seriously

If children live in fear of their adult carers, they will become adults who live in fear. In turn, adults will find it difficult to embrace children's fears mainly because they have too many of their own. For example, a child's fear of the dark will often be dismissed with a laugh or shrugged off as unreal or trivial. This causes the child deep frustration and humiliation. All children need the opportunity to express their fears and concerns, someone to whom they can speak about their innermost thoughts and feelings without fear of judgement or ridicule. Children need to be encouraged to take their feelings seriously, to analyse them and then accept them as their own.

Too many of us respond to children as if they were inanimate objects without feelings. Of course, by encouraging an adult to start getting in touch with a child's feelings, we are asking a 'grown child' to open up their own Pandora's box of raw emotion, which lies dormant or festering in their solar plexus. This potential danger zone may well have been kept tightly shut since childhood. As painful as the process might be, it's time for adults to investigate our own emotions so that we can validate our children's and let them know that their feelings are just as important as ours.

Sexual abuse of children

Children also need to celebrate and enjoy their own physical form. The widespread incidence of sexual abuse suffered by children – which is reported to be as high as 1 in 3 amongst girls and 1 in 7 amongst boys, although it could well be even higher – makes this virtually impossible for many who have been forever shamed and embarrassed by their own bodies and bodily functions. Sexual abuse not only shames the body but also the soul. Children who have experienced any kind of molestation – be it physical or emotional – are scarred for life, and many contemplate suicide as a direct result of the self-loathing and betrayal it engenders.

While the 'Stranger Danger' campaign has done much to raise children's awareness of abuse from outside the family, there has been little done to warn children that they can be just as vulnerable to sexual exploitation within the home. According to the NSPCC, familial sexual abuse is endemic in our society and much more prevalent than ever previously imagined. Their report, 'Child Maltreatment in the UK', released in November 2000, which was based on interviews with nearly 3,000 18–24-year-olds, revealed that 4% had been sexually abused by at least one family member as a child, and that children are twice as likely to be sexually abused by a brother than a father or stepfather. Although there are no national statistics recording the true facts of how widespread sexual abuse is, the charity '1 in 4' suggests that while as many as 25% of children will experience sexual abuse by the age of 18, only 5% of familial abuse is reported to the police, which means that a shocking 95%

is hidden. What's worse is that the average duration of sexual abuse within a family is seven years!

We have to ask ourselves how this tyranny began and why it is allowed to continue. The main reason must be that our culture has been built on denial. Adults refuse to acknowledge that they are capable of harming children, because they would then have to admit that they too were harmed as children. Paedophiles, who were invariably victims of sexual or emotional abuse themselves, transfer their own humiliation and degradation onto their victims. Emotionally detached and incapable of empathy, they operate in a covert way, knowing that the chances of them getting caught are slim. The young victims of abuse are terrified of splitting up the family unit, of disclosing abuse to a mother whose partner may be the abuser, are fearful of being disbelieved and often frozen with shame.

Believing and trusting children

We live in a culture which intrinsically disbelieves and mistrusts children and stifles their voices when they do speak out. Quite simply, adults don't listen well enough to children and their opinions often count for very little. This leaves children feeling intrinsically guilt-ridden, because they've been falsely accused of so many misdemeanours within the family set-up that they grow to believe that almost anything they do will be disapproved of. They've very often been stifled and repressed to the extent that they don't have the confidence or capability to communicate their feelings to the adult populace, and why should they, because this is the very sector of society who are doing the abusing.

Some children must experience a great deal of confusion when it comes to knowing who to trust with their painful secrets. They know that by maintaining a code of silence they will at least keep the peace and not open another can of worms that might bring them even greater pain and anguish. In their innocence and naivety, children implicitly trust adults and find it hard to believe that they would be capable of inflicting harm. But without appropriate role models in their parents, many young people have no conception of what constitutes normal behaviour between adults and children. In addition, many children are raised in homes where the subject of sex is either taboo or a preoccupation, and their value system is based on confused and haphazard messages. All this creates children without any sense of self-worth or personal identity. They operate in a world of vagaries and non-specifics where 'yes' and 'no', 'right' and 'wrong', 'good' and 'bad' are virtually indistinguishable.

We need to create a climate, within our society and our schools, where victims, who have often remained silent and bereft, are listened to, believed and supported. Awareness, prevention and help for victims of abuse should be a central part of a child's education. As it is, our school system is so preoccupied with academic achievement that it makes a child's physical and emotional health a low priority. It virtually ignores the fact that thousands of children are quite incapable of accessing an academic life because they are constantly battling to attain some sort of emotional stability in an effort to mend a broken heart or wounded spirit. Even the most academically gifted can temporarily become disengaged from school work when their parents get a divorce or experience a death in the family.

Potty training

It is not only landmark events within the family that can cause deep emotional trauma. The seemingly simple matter of potty training, which is often insensitively handled by a mother who is desperate to get her child clean, can set up an early emotional rift between mother and child. This process can become a battle of wills causing the child a great deal of unnecessary stress and trauma. Children can reach such a level of aggression that they become hysterical and refuse to be trained. Such an overly controlling approach by the mother is often linked with extreme discipline and the restrictive practice of child masturbation and sex play. For the child, inappropriate potty training can lead to chronic bed-wetting, speech impediments, school failure, an obsession with cleanliness and orderliness as well as a fixation with anal sex.

Mothers need to bear in mind that there is no such thing as the instantly clean child and they have to be extremely sensitive as they make a transition from nurturer to trainer. Just as some children resent their mothers as teachers when they offer help with homework, they can also have an innate resistance to them as toilet trainers! Potty training is a very personal and individual process, and it can take anything from one to four years for children to be in control of their excretory functions. If the experience can be shared with a teddy bear or a doll then it takes a lot of pressure off the child. Potty training is best achieved by pleasurable means at the pace of the child, not the adult.

Feeding children and eating disorders

Parents' need to control their children can also manifest itself in what they eat. Since mothers have control over what is fed to their children, food intake can easily take on an emotional dimension. In many homes, food is unconsciously regarded as feeding the emotions as well as providing sustenance and nourishment for the body. There are some mothers who project their fears and insecurities onto their children when it comes to feeding them. In the knowledge that they are often incapable of loving them through their souls, some mothers indulge their children through their mouths. What children are not receiving in love is being forced upon them in food. We certainly wouldn't force-feed an adult, but that's exactly what we do to our children. In return, some children who are keen to placate their overanxious mothers will often overeat and even stuff themselves to capacity. Fat children are rarely suffering from a genetic disorder. They are much more likely to have inherited bad eating habits from their emotionally-fragile parents.

If we are to avoid eating disorders such as anorexia, bulimia and compulsive overeating, which are usually the direct result of negative attitudes to food within a family's emotional make-up, we need to instil in our children early on that they need to 'eat to live' and not 'live to eat'. Food is a source of nourishment and not a way of dealing with emotional trauma. It is widely acknowledged that one of the most effective ways of setting children on the right path to healthy eating habits is to breastfeed as and when babies need it. It is believed to encourage good long-term habits of only eating when hungry and eating just enough to satisfy bodily needs. As children mature, mealtimes need to be as peaceful as possible. Children need to be encouraged to eat only what they like and not be forced to eat everything on their plates. They instinctively know what they might be allergic to, or what will make them sick or hyperactive, and will usually avoid such foods. If mothers constantly impose their views about the right types of food for a balanced diet, their fussing and insistence will probably do more damage to their children's emotional development than it could ever do to their physical health.

Mothers also need to understand that the way they relate to food is often copied by their children. Mothers who are obsessed with healthy eating can create obsessional eating

41

in their children. By being on a constant diet and ballooning up and down, they are also not very good role models. They're basically saying, 'It's fine for me to be obsessed by everything I eat but you certainly mustn't follow my example!'

Later on, children who have not learnt good eating habits will invariably become adults who use food as a source of comfort and an emotional crutch. Bingeing is often linked with a yearning for love. In the absence of the real thing, a person will receive love from a bar of chocolate or a tub of ice cream. It is all a part of reverting to the oral gratification of babyhood as children search for the unconditional love they never received.

Living in a material world

Children are not only overindulged with food, they can also be victims of consumerism. In a bid to prove ourselves good parents and perpetuate an illusion of the perfect childhood, we often encourage children to acquire and accumulate all the latest toys and gadgets in the belief that materialism is synonymous with love. But a recent study by Abbey National revealed that 50% of Britain's 7–9-year-olds believe they get too many Christmas presents, and four out of five have toys they never play with. This research might well indicate that an addiction to retail therapy is essentially a parental problem.

Parents need to be honest with their children if they are experiencing financial problems and let them know that they may not get everything they ask for. It is often the case that children who are indulged are not always appreciative of the sacrifices their parents make to give them everything they want. What's ironic is that young children are often more interested in the packaging of a gift, and a thoughtful gift can be of far more sentimental value than an expensive one. This Christmas, my son gained endless hours of pleasure from a plastic spinning top found in an inexpensive Christmas cracker.

Ideally, we need to treat our children as if every day was Christmas day or a birthday by giving the gift of love. Children need to be told and to feel how wonderful, beautiful and special they are every day of the year. They are then less likely to crave material gifts on a particular day, especially Christmas Day, which, after all, is the only official holiday of the year that we set aside for the celebration of someone else's birthday!

Behind closed doors

As we have seen, there is a constant power struggle influencing most aspects of the parent–child relationship. This must be because parents' power over their children is unequivocally accepted by society as their sole domain. With absolute ownership rights, they are allowed to do exactly what they like in the privacy of their own home and beyond. Just what kind of terror is inflicted on innocent children behind closed doors does not bear thinking about. We only have to observe the abusive behaviour of some parents towards their children when they are merely expressing boredom or frustration in a supermarket because they're getting less attention than a shopping list, or visit a park or housing estate and witness the wild rantings of a parent screaming at their child at play (both controlled and modified forms of what goes on at home), to realise the suffering of children behind closed doors.

In an omnipotent way, many parents assume the roles of king and queen within the family domain, while their children are expected to respond as loyal subjects of the realm. But surely children cannot be considered the sole property of two people who can manipulate and bend their minds, bodies and spirits at will. While children may come through their parents, they cannot be considered their property or possession. They are only lent to their carers for a short while and, as separate souls with their own unique destinies, they deserve the highest respect.

It seems to me that society needs to take a more active role in monitoring the welfare of every child within the context of the family of humankind. It often takes a crisis, such as an extreme case of physical or sexual abuse, before anyone champions the well-being of our children. What's worse is that hardly anyone seems to be taking responsibility for the vicious circle of neglect. But if it is not reversed, yet another generation will automatically inflict the same unresolved pain on their children.

Children are capable of so much more than we give them credit for, and yet we often treat them with little more than contempt. But if, as Froebel said, 'In the children lies the seed corn of the future,' the basic disrespect of children is not a trivial matter. It impacts every aspect of our lives. We only have to look at the childhood experiences of some of the world's most evil dictators to know that a humiliated and degraded child has the potential to become a warmonger of the highest order. Unless society accepts that warfare is nurtured in infancy we will never be free of its scourge.

Children have strong imitative responses when it comes to witnessing acts of physical or verbal abuse. If they are subjected to hostility and anxiety during infancy, they will not have the emotional resources to cope with stressful situations as adults. They will be more likely to exhibit extreme reactions in a crisis, such as excessive compliance or extreme aggression. Compliance can lead to the victim mentality while aggression can lead to the bully mentality. Children will store any violent incident directly inflicted on themselves, or witnessed between their parents, in an unconscious memory bank. Even if children don't imitate what they experience or see in childhood, they will almost certainly feel compelled to do so later on. In hindsight, they will come to regard these violent episodes as normal patterns of behaviour and could well re-enact them as adults.

The vital role of play

Play can have a significant part in dealing with children's concerns over aggression and any other physical or emotional problems they might be experiencing. Through the use of symbolism, it allows them to confront and solve problems that they would not normally be able to cope with in real life. It also offers heightened awareness of their environment and allows them the opportunity for greater control of their lives. Children attach a great deal of importance to their parents' participation in the experience. They not only enjoy the validation of their favourite activity, but like the idea of parent and child coming together on equal terms. The collaborative element helps break down all sorts of barriers, bridging the gap between their two worlds, and allowing parents to gain greater insight into their children's emotional needs. While many parents regard playful activities as a waste of time and will make any number of excuses not to spend time with their children, the benefits are enormous. Through their more leisurely pace, children can help adults to slow down and rediscover the magic of childhood.

While children often welcome parental involvement during play, they tend to resent help with physical milestones such as crawling, walking, climbing and speaking. They want to take things at their own pace as they seek independence. As adults, we tend to take short cuts but, while these may be good for us, they are not so good for children. Generally, adults seem to be irritated by the slowness of children, but we need to understand that they operate at an entirely different pace. Since children tend to live eternally in the present, their internal rhythmic patterns are quite distinct from those of adults and need to be honoured as such.

It is always better if children can teach themselves by their own active experience. Parents need to be aware that it is better not to interfere unnecessarily in their children's development. As young people learn from their own experience, they need to do things for themselves without persuasion or force. Children often misbehave because they are reacting to adults who are impeding their natural physical development, preventing them from a creative activity which is vital for character building.

Toys as weapons of aggression

In much the same way as play is acknowledged as a child's way of making sense of the world, their toys represent strong symbols of self-expression and identity. When children are encouraged to play with guns, tanks and the machinery of war they are unconsciously preparing themselves for an aggressive and combative adulthood. This is not to suggest that, by playing with a toy gun, all children will want to become soldiers or transfer to a real gun in adulthood and use it against others. But there will be some children who, in the absence of good parental guidance, may get entirely the wrong message. Some children could feel that because a toy weapon is sanctioned by their parents, whose judgement they implicitly trust, they have been given the green light to regard it as a means by which to attack others or to defend themselves. While the outcome is relatively harmless when it comes to interaction with childhood peers, they might well progress to the real thing and use it against anyone who crosses them in later life. If weapons did not exist in play form, they would almost certainly not exist in real form.

There are those who argue that toy guns and other implements of war are an integral part of a child's symbolic play, an outlet for expressing aggression, and that their prohibition might actually increase children's anger and frustration because they see other children enjoying their use and the movie industry glorifying them. Another argument which is often voiced in defence of their use is that unless children, particularly boys, are allowed to nurture their innate aggression, there will be no military force to take on another Hitler, who, incidentally, was allegedly subjected to extreme emotional abuse at the hands of his dictatorial father.

But, no matter how accepted and widespread their use (according to the British police, 1 in 3 criminals under the age of 25 now owns a gun or can get their hands on one and 3 million are held illegally in the UK, which is double the number held 10 years ago), guns are potentially lethal weapons. Surely we need to be giving a clear and uncompromising message to our children that it's time to disarm and lay down all types of weapons. It's my belief that if all children had their emotional needs met and were dissuaded from following gender stereotypes, no one would be interested in making or using weapons and they would soon become obsolete. On a larger scale, if no one was capable or willing to instigate or fight a war, the world would be at peace.

Repressed childhood feelings

Through the eyes of a child, it must seem that adults hold all the trump cards. But young people have an uncanny habit of getting their own back for any physical or emotional abuse they suffered. As adults, they will almost certainly seek a release, which is invariably unconscious. Extreme repressed childhood feelings are either taken out on others – society, family or parents – in the form of antisocial behaviour such as emotional cruelty, violence or crime, or on ourselves, in self-destructive forms such as drug addiction, alcoholism or mental illness.

For many more, childhood injustices can have a tremendous impact on an adult's social interaction, especially in intimate relationships. Men tend to idealise their mothers and put aside any direct blame for the intimidation they suffered. Instead, they project their anger onto other women as they seek revenge. Women, on the other hand, tend to get revenge through their children, inflicting and reinforcing the pain and anguish of their own childhood.

And still we continue to propagate an idealistic view of childhood. In a society which tends to protect the adult and blame the juvenile, we live under the illusion that every child has an idyllic upbringing free of fear, anxiety and stress. Even children tend to perpetuate the myth by operating an inbuilt defence mechanism which helps them to block out the truth of what actually happened. But unless adults are truly conscious of their repressed childhood experiences, the burden of denial and unresolved action will stunt their individual growth and live on from generation to generation.

Chapter Two

Education Today

The business of school

Just as our family system is fundamentally flawed and dysfunctional so, too, is our school system. It rarely has anything to do with who a child is in terms of their feelings and emotions, but much more to do with what they are expected to attain within a pressure pot of achievement and conformity. As schools expand and become more enterprising, they are no longer regarded as simply centres of learning. They are also business centres with a commercial dimension. The governing body is the board of directors, the head teacher the managing director, the senior teachers the duty managers, the class teachers the line managers and the pupils the production line. It's not surprising that some children feel like they're on a conveyor belt.

Competition is now so keen between schools as they vie for funding to improve and expand that they are increasingly conscious of building a strong corporate identity. The most significant ways forward are to do well in an Ofsted inspection, improve national test scores and elevate the school's position in the league tables. By doing all that, a school is judged to be successful. But where do such pragmatic criteria leave schools in areas of social deprivation as they support pupils with little or no parental backing? Many are being equated to failing businesses and are doomed to be singled out as failing schools. Ultimately, it's the children who miss out because if their school is 'named and shamed' they will become even more demoralised and regard themselves as part of the failure.

According to The United Nations Children's Fund, one in five children in Britain lives in poverty. The United Kingdom's high levels of poverty are comparable to those in Mexico, The United States and Italy. UNICEF identifies a definite correlation between children who grow up in poverty and those who experience learning difficulties, school dropouts, drug problems, crime and unemployment. It is hardly surprising that schools who support pupils from families living on densely populated working-class estates, surviving on or below the poverty line, are doomed to be at the lower end of the academic ladder.

Such schools and their pupils need help and support, not further condemnation and rejection. Their levels of performance simply cannot be equated with schools in wealthy, leafy suburbs with a middle-class intake.

The pressure pot of school life

The relentless drive to boost up targets and succeed in examinations has never been greater. The demand for children to gain qualifications comes not just from schools and teachers but from the government, the media, employers and parents. Pressure from all these sources to achieve and behave according to rigid and inflexible guidelines can leave children in a constant state of feeling flawed. They often give up because they feel they can never win. On completing a self-assessment form at the end of year 5, my son's response, when asked whether he was pleased with his behaviour in school and if he could improve on it, was, 'No, because I can't do anything right!' What's really sad is that hardly anyone seems to be protecting, listening to or defending the rights of children who are daily subjected to this intensive education programme, even when they face burnout.

One in five children suffers from a mental illness and many more experience aggression, drug abuse, bed-wetting, sleeplessness, eating disorders and depression. As many as one in three children experience bullying at some time in their school life. School phobia is on the increase as more and more children complain of intense competition, having to struggle with work that is beyond them, being kick-started, force-fed a curriculum that bears little relation to real life, and the restrictive routine of sitting at a desk for most of the day without adequate physical exercise. The child psychologist, Maria Montessori, had a particular aversion to regular classrooms and spoke of 'Children, like butterflies mounted on pins, are fastened each to his place.'

On returning to school after a recent Christmas break, a teacher shared the response she'd had from an informal discussion with a 'top' year 9 group about what the holidays meant to them. She told me that they'd unanimously agreed that being on holiday meant 'happiness' and returning to school meant 'sadness'. My colleague added, 'I honestly believe that for most children school is a painful endurance test!'

Homework

Not only are many children subjected to a heavy workload during the day, they are then expected to do several hours' homework in the evening. This can be the straw that breaks the camel's back. Even repressed Victorian children, who were under constant threat of canings and beatings, marched through the streets in protest at having to do homework.

While it might be appropriate for GCSE students, homework can extend the school day to such an extent that some children have little or no time for leisure activities and an opportunity to recharge their batteries. The introduction of school homework clubs is good for working parents, but puts pressure on children to extend their school day when they could be relaxing in a different environment.

Homework can be punishing for both children and parents – children, because they're tired and lack enthusiasm, and parents, because, more often than not, they're the ones who have to ensure it's being done and may well be called upon to help with it. This can put a lot of stress on the parent/child relationship, because the child often resents the parent in teaching role. In some cases, parents feel inadequate to help if the task is not understood or is intellectually beyond them.

No time to stand and stare

Not only is the school day getting longer, so, too, is the number of years a child spends in education now that four-year-olds have the opportunity to get on the academic treadmill. There are many educationists who believe the longer we can delay formal education the better. A number favour the Scandinavian tradition of starting school at seven, which most child psychologists refer to as 'the age of reason'. Up until then, they argue, children have plenty to learn through the exploration of their senses and feelings in a range of creative play activities. By introducing under fives to state schools and the 3Rs, we might be further alienating children from formal education and robbing them of their individual right to just be.

It seems that the sheer enjoyment of doing 'nothing' has all but vanished from children's lives. Their every waking moment has to be filled with doing something. Many of us are beginning to ask the simple question, 'Whatever happened to play and childhood?'

The opportunity for children to stand and stare, to relax and empty their minds, to contemplate and reflect, to role-play in game playing are activities that are no longer encouraged.

Driven to the edge

The increase in the number of tests young people now have to endure is certainly not helping them to enjoy the learning experience. Some schools have undergone as many as four national tests in less than a decade. Every year, ChildLine talks to at least 800 pupils who report that exams are a major source of stress. While half the calls come from GCSE students, more than a hundred are from pupils under the age of 14. Surely this indicates that we're placing too much emphasis on the outcome rather than the process of education, too much rides on test results and not enough on continuous assessment. If we're not careful, not only will many children be put off education for life, more will be driven to take their lives.

While we cannot always be sure of the motives for suicide – adolescent depression can be triggered not only by exams but also hormonal changes, relationships with parents and the opposite sex, parental divorce and drug-related problems – a consistently high rate amongst the young over the past decade must partly be attributed to increased stress at school. According to Samaritans, UK-wide in 2001 alone, there were 27 suicides among the under-14s and 660 among 15–25-year-olds, with young men being particularly at risk. The lack of opportunity for non-academic young men to pursue an apprenticeship is certainly alienating them, and having a negative effect on their morale and self-worth. The fact that Britain has the worst truancy problem in Europe, and 10,400 children were permanently excluded from school in 1999, is a clear indication of the general malaise and disillusionment felt by many young people today.

Some of the common complaints that I frequently hear from high-school pupils are that while they enjoy break times, socialising with their friends, school trips and after-school activities, the academic side is mostly boring, restricting and uncreative. They complain that there's far too much emphasis on academic achievement, which causes competition and alienation from their peers.

Many believe that education is incompatible with and irrelevant to what they experience outside school and that it doesn't prepare them for their future needs. They say that disruptive kids get all the attention and prevent them from learning. They feel teachers need to treat students as equals, or at least with respect, instead of patronising them. They are fed up with being accused and blamed for things they haven't done. They want teachers to stop labelling them, overreacting and taking things out on them when they're in a bad mood. They complain of too many lessons which involve copying off the board, a lack of resources, the rigidity of school uniform, and the need for a few more privileges and quiet times. But, above all, they believe that school is stuck in a time warp.

A Victorian ethic

In this last regard, they are almost certainly right. While seventeenth-century school children boldly took it upon themselves to defend their rights by being armed and were even responsible for violent mutinies at school, our present-day model of mass schooling is far more aligned with that adopted by the Victorian middle classes. Education was then used as a means of controlling the urban poor and stemming a rise in juvenile delinquency. With a strict social regime based on repression and conformity, the Victorians became obsessed with containing the masses through education.

While it succeeded in squashing social rebellion, then, it is hardly a blueprint for a country that's moved on a century. And yet teachers are still telling pupils what to do and how to do it and assessing it all on the basis of a potential A. The doctrines of 'being seen and not heard' and always 'doing as you're told by your elders and betters', though firmly rooted in the Victorian era, still form the basis of an accepted code of practice between adults and children.

In accordance with the Victorian ethic of 'don't do as I do but do as I say', millions of children are the victims of constant verbal subjugation and a feeling of being browbeaten. In the name of discipline, many adults, often quite unconsciously, speak to – or rather at – their children in an unrelentingly stern or gruff voice. Very often the only relief is the occasional direct or inferred slur of 'stupid', 'thick' or 'ignorant'. Some adults address their dogs in a more respectful way.

Intrinsic goodness

You can undermine human beings in this manner for only so long before they begin to believe what they're hearing. As the self-fulfilling prophecy kicks in, children start to act according to their label. Even the most vigilant adults can fall into bad and lazy speech patterns which were perpetuated in their own childhood conditioning, e.g. a 'good boy' or 'good girl' label can have a negative connotation because the opposite of good is bad, and children then believe they have the potential to be bad. They know they cannot constantly meet the adults' criteria of being 'good'. It is only a matter of time before they will be 'bad'. We have to let our children know that they are all intrinsically good and that this is an unconditional belief which is not dependent on how they act or behave.

Children who are nagged at home are often offered little respite at school. There is no doubt that teachers, like parents, have their patience pushed to the limits. The policing side of a teacher's job is arguably the most stressful aspect. In order to cope with crowd control, teachers often adopt 'a teacher's voice' which, like a drill sergeant, is typically strident and unrelenting in tone. While a short, sharp command may get the desired response in the short term, constant verbal confrontation, based on intimidation, is a major part of the alienation that pupils feel from their teachers. After a while, pupils switch off from what is being demanded of them as it all becomes a monotonous and meaningless monologue.

Authentic teachers

Children have an uncanny radar system when it comes to knowing whether teachers are being themselves or staying in role to maintain a persona of aloofness and detachment. Just as pupils appreciate the opportunity to be themselves, they like teachers to be themselves. They want their teachers to reveal themselves as real people and dispense with the facade that many hide behind. For this to happen, teachers need to be aware of what it is to be authentic, to be truly honest and open in the presence of children.

Unfortunately, many teachers are only able to offer their pupils an occasional glimpse of their essence. Out of fear of losing control and respect, they often feel safer speaking in stern and formal tones when communicating with children.

Pupils must be perplexed when they observe teachers switch from speaking to a member of staff with civility and respect to addressing a child in a cold and disrespectful tone.

It can be particularly bewildering for a pupil to be on the receiving end of sarcasm, a subtle but damning weapon that some teachers use against children. The sting is no less painful than getting the cane, and the memory can be just as deeply etched in a child's psyche, if not more so.

Vengeful teachers

The powerful effect of a teacher's words goes deep, and they will often be remembered throughout a child's life. Even the use of nicknames or diminutives and tags such as 'sunshine' or 'sweetheart' can cause resentment and a feeling of being undervalued. Children much prefer to be addressed by their proper first name. One of the most important jobs for a teacher is to learn the names of their pupils as soon as possible. It is an essential building block for a good relationship between teachers and children.

But it's the tone of an adult's voice, rather than what is actually being said, which has the most lasting impression on a child. My sister, who was caught singing along the corridors of her secondary school, will bear witness to that. One day a senior teacher came up behind her and scathingly remarked, 'Don't you ever let me catch you singing in the corridors again!' At just thirteen, she was in need of greater emotional support than usual because our father had just died. I can remember her telling me that the tone of that remark felt like she'd been punched in the solar plexus.

Fortunately, there was an English teacher who was able to put her wise to the fact that the powers that be already had it in for the 'arty' students, who had to work twice as hard not to get picked on. While my sister will never forget the painful impact of that teacher's words, she was able to fulfil her ambition of becoming a professional singer/songwriter. There are other less resilient children who have been mortally wounded by a teacher's insensitive words. Some can feel forever shamed by a cutting comment which was regarded by the teacher as nothing more than a throwaway remark.

I, too, can recall several teachers from my sensitive teenage years whose vindictive words have left deep emotional scars. There was a particular textiles teacher who seemed to take delight in berating my poor skills as a needlewoman, a PE teacher who taunted me when I dropped a catch on the rounders field and my private piano teacher, who ritualistically threatened to demote me from playing her grand piano to the upright if I didn't practise harder. As a child, they made me feel inadequate and shamed.

This kind of intimidation and lack of patience or restraint by teachers has to be a form of unconsciously avenging themselves for what was projected onto them by their teachers. But this can only breed and perpetuate further anxiety and fear, causing young people to clam up and render learning dead in its tracks. Intimidation only serves to arrest children's development. It does nothing for their confidence or self-esteem. It is not until we become adults that we realise we were not the ones with the problem!

Above all, children expect teachers to be in control of their emotions and not to lose their temper when they feel they're losing control of a situation. Confrontation can add fuel to an already incendiary situation. There's nothing more destabilising, or amusing, to a group of children than to see a teacher who is out of control and acting like a child. Unfortunately, this is exactly what is happening much of the time, because the truth is that many teachers are adult children acting out their own childhood experiences with all the unresolved accusation, anger and aggression that accompanied them.

Self-aware teachers

It is only the teachers who had a comparatively functional and trauma-free childhood, or those who have actively sought help to resolve their childhood issues, who will be equipped to handle children with the care and respect they deserve and need. Teachers will only be able to embrace and celebrate the real feelings and emotions of the children in their care by increasing their own self-awareness. This can be nurtured through an in-depth understanding of child psychology, a course in counselling including interpersonal and assertiveness skills, coupled with at least a year of personal psychotherapy to resolve childhood issues. I believe such preparation needs to be integral to the studies of a student teacher.

Unless teachers understand their own emotional make-up, they will be unlikely to recognise and deal with the extensive range of feelings and emotions expressed by their pupils. The better they are able to understand their own behaviour and responses, the better they will be able to understand and deal with the behaviour of children. In the same way, the more tolerant teachers are of their own shortcomings, the more tolerant they will be of children's. Despite many years of teaching experience and personal development, I am still overawed as I enter a classroom full of children and look out on a sea of psyches and try to reconcile them with my own.

At least we have moved away from the concept of 'training' teachers. I've always been concerned with the term 'teacher training', because it implies instructing and accumulating a body of facts, or the performance of repetitious operations without understanding the underlying principles. Since teaching is an art rather than an acquired skill, and teachers and children are individuals, to train all children in the same mould would rob them of their individuality. Training is an entirely inappropriate term, as it implies indoctrination. Indoctrination aims to close the mind whereas education aims to open and develop it. As the adage goes, the mind, like a parachute, works best when it is open.

Teaching with empathy

The personality of the teacher is arguably their greatest teaching aid, far more important than their academic qualifications. Every day of my teaching life I hear children say, 'I don't like the subject because I don't like the teacher!' A teacher who is able to offer a degree of love and compassion is far more useful to a child than a teacher with a Ph.D. in quantum physics. Children have very little interest in teachers' own knowledge or the facts that they wish to impart. They sense that it is not the job of teachers to enforce ideas upon them but to provide creative energy to fuel and channel their own individual and creative impulses. If this can be done in a kind and empathetic way then all the better. A polite and kind teacher, with a well-modulated but firm voice, who shows dignity in a stressful situation is not only a good role model but is likely to operate a serene and productive classroom.

While a powerful tool, it is important that the personality of the teacher does not dominate the class. Teachers need to share themselves without imposing their presence. A non-judgmental and selfless person, who is in touch with their own 'inner child', can be far more valuable to the teaching profession than an ambitious high-flyer who places self-interest above their pupils' well-being. The teacher needs to have an unconditionally high regard for every pupil. With the wonder and pleasure of the child as their motivation, teachers can transform children's lives. I have seen pupils metamorphose with just a modicum of attention and encouragement. We can only imagine how far children's spirits might soar if every teacher was in touch with their own feelings and emotions and had the capability and resources to have their pupils' emotional interests truly at heart.

Of course, teachers need to be passionate about their subject matter so that they can instil passion in their pupils. If children do not enjoy what they are learning, or are bored, it is the responsibility of the teacher to search for more innovative ways of presenting a subject. It is not enough for a teacher to operate on a physical plane as a distributor of knowledge, they also need the spiritual and sensual dimensions which will help them to stimulate and sustain children's creative development.

Children on the move

It is also important for teachers to be aware that the children they are teaching are already restricted and at their mercy – mentally, in terms of the content and time constraints imposed in a lesson and, physically, because they are expected to remain seated in an appointed place for the duration of a particular lesson or, sometimes, for a good part of the school day. I have always questioned the concept of expecting children to sit at desks, sometimes perfectly still without fidgeting. These are supposed to be prerequisites for concentration. This may be true for short periods at a time, but the passivity that is asked of children for long periods of the day is unnatural and must be held accountable as the primary cause of deviant behaviour in the classroom. Gifted children seem to find it particularly difficult to sit still.

While it suits teachers for children to be quiet and compliant, young people have a natural compunction and predisposition for movement. It helps the development of spatial concepts. My twin brother found it impossible to sit at a desk for longer than a few minutes. While his need to move around the room was a constant source of irritation to his infant teachers, it probably signified nothing more than an inbred impetus for movement. In my experience, children tend to judge the difference between a comfortable and an uncomfortable ambience in a classroom by how much liberty they're offered. The opportunity to stand up, move around and communicate with their peers is an important part of their school day.

School reports and labelling

If we are to believe in the mightiness of the pen, then school reports can be another source of anguish for young children. Quite recently, a 12-year-old Leeds boy was discovered by his mother hanging from his bunk bed with his dressing-gown cord wrapped around his neck. Just minutes before he'd taken his life, he'd read his school report, which stated that he had 'the attention span of a goldfish'.

While there was no proof that this remark had any direct link with his suicide, it is worthy of consideration. As a spokesperson for Leeds Council who was commenting on the matter said, 'An incident of this type shows the need to reflect carefully on the impact our words have.'

Although most teachers show restraint and consideration in their written judgements of a child, many use loaded comments such as 'tries hard but could do better', 'lacks concentration' and 'seeks attention' in place of more damning comments which might enrage a parent. If children are not directly aware of the inference, they are confused by it. Children are much more likely to respond to constructive criticism than unsubstantiated innuendo.

By constantly labelling pupils as disruptive or incompetent, they begin to accept these labels and live up to them. Just as children inherit, or acquire, a social position within the family structure, such as achiever, rebel or scapegoat, and learn to act out that role even though they may dislike it, a school pupil will develop a self-concept such as boffin, dunce, victim or clown. If children are assigned a negative role, their self-concept mirrors it. They begin to see themselves in terms of it and act accordingly. Once they assume a negative mantle, they will often carry it through their school life and beyond. It may have little to do with who they actually are and can greatly limit their potential.

Some children are so deprived of status through low academic performance that they develop a deviant and antisocial response to school as a coping or covering-up mechanism. They are either ostracised from the rest of the class or gravitate to pupils of the same low status and develop a splinter group in a bid to elevate their status. But, more often than not, this results in more rather than less challenging behaviour.

One of the most important and difficult roles of the teacher is to recognise the different roles being played out by the children in their class. In this regard, the teacher is the paradigm of the parent. Just as a pre-school child takes on a role which is often created and developed by a parent, a pupil takes on a role which is rooted and nurtured in the way a teacher reacts and responds to that child. Children look to their parents for guidance at home and to their teachers for guidance at school.

They trust them both as arbiters of fair play, sound judgement and keen perception; at least they do at first, until their trust is broken and their hopes dashed.

During the course of their day, children seek a consistent transition from parents to teachers and back to parents. Unfortunately, this is rarely what they will experience. While they may be lucky enough to be understood and cherished by either their parents or their teachers, it is more likely that they will be misunderstood and degraded by both. This can leave them alone in the world, feeling that they have no allies and no one to whom they can express their feelings and emotions. It is only when children become adults that they are able to analyse the family and school system they came from and recognise the roles they were compelled to play out for their very survival. By then it is often too late to reinvent and rekindle the real self which can be lost forever.

Reading projection

One of the most important aspects of children's personalities that teachers need to understand is that they often project the exact opposite of what they are actually feeling. If children are prone to bragging and bravado they are often feeling deeply insecure. If children are rude to adults it is often a way of letting them know that they feel misunderstood and undervalued. If children are quiet and introverted or prone to extroversion they might be carrying a huge burden of shame or guilt. If children have temper tantrums they could be expressing the anger which they are not permitted to express at home. And yet all these perfectly natural responses can be regarded as antisocial behaviour within the context of institutional life.

As antisocial as these emotional outbursts may appear to be to an insensitive or desensitised adult, they are actually an extremely healthy response to an act of injustice or painful event and show a rather mature reaction to a deep-seated dilemma within the child's psyche. If children are

64

brave enough to lay their feelings on the line, the very least teachers can do is to respect their courage and allow them to break the rules occasionally without getting reprimanded or punished.

For example, if children arrive at school on a Monday morning in a bad mood because they've had a difficult weekend at home, they may be asked to stand outside the classroom to cool down, but this gives them the message that being angry is not socially acceptable. They feel shamed and intimidated and resent being excluded from their peer group at a time when they most need their support. Such pupils need to be embraced and accepted by the class and their teacher, to be given the opportunity to explain why they are so upset or to sit quietly and reflect on the events that led up to their emotional outburst. They certainly do not need to be rejected and excluded.

Expressing emotion in the classroom

Unfortunately, more often than not, children who express emotional responses are likely to get reprimanded or punished because they are not conforming to the model of 'normal behaviour' which has been set by the teacher. But if teachers want all the children to act in a way which conforms to an ideal, they need to negotiate the terms of such a contract with all the members of the class, taking each pupil's emotional make-up into account. Every child needs to agree to a set of ground rules which are negotiated by the class, such as listening to and respecting other people, taking responsibility for your own actions, keeping agreements and not hurting anyone verbally or physically. Only then will each pupil come to understand the teacher's definition of what is appropriate in the classroom situation. With assertive and calm reminders of the ground rules by the teacher, children start to take responsibility for their own behaviour and the ethos of a class can change dramatically.

Adults need to own up that it is very often their inadequate parenting or teaching which causes deviant behaviour in children. It is only by facing the reality of their own poor behaviour that they can take steps to improve it. They need to understand that children learn inappropriate behaviour through imitation or reinforcement. Some children have not been taught to discriminate what behaviour is appropriate to a certain situation. Those children who have had inadequate parenting will need warmth and support, as opposed to condemnation and punishment, in learning how to trust adults and deal with social contexts at school. This can be particularly poignant for only children, who are often the centre of their parents' universe and tend to live mostly in an adult world. They will often be confused by what is expected of them because they straddle the worlds of the adult and the child.

Deep down, all children want to please their teacher, but the experiences of their pre-school years often render them incapable of behaving in an acceptable way within the dynamics of a classroom situation. No matter what they project, they probably find school life torturous and tortuous.

The fact that there have been several years of intense input from parents before a child even reaches school is an important consideration. It is quite difficult for a teacher to influence or reverse a pattern of inappropriate behaviour once a child starts school. But parents often expect teachers to rectify their inadequate parenting and turn the challenging behaviour of their children around as if by magic. Even though it is not their direct responsibility, teachers often feel obliged to transform the underdeveloped social skills of children who have not come through the counterdependency stage of their toddler years and have failed to establish an independent identity in the pre-school stage.

The number of children who suffer from this kind of arrested development tends to be between 15% and 20% in every class. (Most teachers can just about cope with this number. A higher percentage can become intolerable.) Often dubbed 'the disruptive element', this group of children exhibit emotional and social problems which can make life for the teacher and the other class members very difficult indeed. The fact that the many are disrupted by the behaviour of the few is one of the most frustrating parts of school life, for both teachers and pupils. As things stand, the only solution, other than exclusion, is to try and redress their poor start in life by nurturing them with warmth and support. It is very important that their acceptable behaviour is reinforced by praise or reward.

One day I was teaching art to a year 7 group and asked them if they'd enjoyed art lessons at junior school. Most of the children said they had, but one boy, who had found it quite difficult to settle and focus throughout the lesson, stated that he'd hated every moment of his time at junior school because the teachers never stopped picking on him. When I asked him if that was really how he felt, he replied, 'No miss, that's what I knew!'

He sobbed inconsolably for five minutes. Here was a 12-year-old child who already felt betrayed by the education system.

Teachers as trusted role models

At the root of the teacher–pupil relationship is trust. Children desperately need role models they can trust. But for teachers to trust children, they must trust themselves. The problem is that many teachers were told as children that they could not be trusted. One of the biggest challenges for teachers is to transcend the distrust they experienced and replace it with unconditional trust for the pupils in their care. Teachers owe it to their pupils not to betray their trust. Every time a child is disappointed in a teacher's response concerning matters of trust, it not only gnaws away at the child's faith in the education system but also damages their self-belief.

Just like the medical profession, teachers need to abandon their godlike image of invincibility as the model of absolute truth and virtue and let their pupils know that they are not the fountains of all knowledge, but human beings capable of mistakes and with the capacity to say, 'I was wrong and I'm sorry.' Teachers also need to dispense with their model of the perfect pupil. It may be easier to deal with a child who is agreeable and pliant, diligent and undemanding, but the nonconformists, with more provocative and demanding behaviour traits, need to be validated too. At the moment, there is too much distinction between teachers' pets and teachers' pests!

Boys' development

Boys can suffer quite badly when a teacher makes a bright, well-behaved girl with social graces the model of perfection and aspiration. When they first start school, boys already feel intimidated by girls because they tend to read and write earlier. In the past, there has been a tendency for boys to catch up later, but that is no longer the case. Currently, their more academic female peers are outshining them at GCSEs, not only in literacy, but also in maths and sciences. While they shrug off the concept of 'girl power', I have perceived that boys are embarrassed and emasculated by it. They are much more likely to be in tune with the idea of 'equal power for all children'! It certainly seems that our education system favours the temperament of girls, who appear not only to have a greater capacity for conformity and hard work but, more significantly, a propensity for emotional maturity.

I am convinced that the root cause of boys' academic underachievement, mostly in written and verbal communication, is that while girls are encouraged to be more emotionally literate at an early age, boys are left emotionally illiterate. Very early on, girls are taught to be expressive of their own feelings and sensitive to others, while boys are expected to be self-reliant and in denial of their feelings. Boys are more likely to be encouraged to maintain a stiff upper lip and discouraged from crying. But all human beings need to cry, for various reasons. Tears release endorphins, which block pain receptors and produce an essential anaesthetic to help us cope with the worst of our grief. Boys tend to keep their vulnerabilities disguised or hidden behind a rigid mask of self-reliance. This often puts them on the defensive and leaves them feeling alone in the world.

It's no wonder that boys get frustrated and exhibit more challenging behaviour in the classroom. But the male tradition of isolation needs to be resolved if we are to curb the adolescent drug and alcohol problem as well as boys' general attitude towards sex. Lack of emotional maturity often encourages boys to indulge in the sexual act purely for pleasure, without any interest in love or responsibility toward the female. It can also lead to sex addiction, where sex is used as a mood-altering 'drug' or as a release of tension caused by being cut off from feelings. In my experience, boys are equally as sensitive as girls and long to be connected to their feelings. In a state of emotional withdrawal, many are racked by inner turmoil and confusion. Frustrated by having to restrain and contain their emotions, they resort to projecting them into various of impulsive forms of hyperactive antisocial behaviour.

It is interesting to note that two to four times as many boys are diagnosed with attention deficit hyperactivity disorder

(ADHD) as are girls, which means that there is likely to be one hyperactive boy in every class. This condition may be the result of a brain chemistry disorder or, to some degree, it might be attributed to unresolved emotional turmoil within a boy's psyche. While ADHD is supposed to indicate an attention deficit caused by lack of concentration, it might well, more accurately, indicate that the child is not getting enough attention, especially if the father is either physically absent, which is the case in up to a third of British homes, or emotionally unavailable.

Hyperactivity

When considering all children with attention deficit problems and hyperactivity, diet cannot be ignored. Many go to school without breakfast and their blood sugar may be abnormally low, which affects brain function. When they do eat, most young people consume far too much junk food, including sweet sticky foods, chocolate, chips and caffeine-laden soft drinks. These types of foods can also affect sleep and cause allergies, respiratory problems and anaemia as well as behavioural difficulties. If children were encouraged daily to eat three balanced meals – a diet rich in protein, slow-burning carbohydrates, plenty of fresh fruit and vegetables and free of refined ingredients – their minds would be far more alert and they would also be able to deal with their emotions more effectively.

It is also important to consider the phenomenon of 'hyper-parenting', where children are being driven so hard that they barely have time to draw breath. So-called 'hothousing' of children, who are encouraged to join every available sports club, learn an instrument, attend all after-school activities as well as achieve in the classroom, can leave them reeling and stressed out. Such a punishing schedule might well contribute to poor concentration, hyperactivity and other stress-related illnesses such as headaches, gastric ulcers and, in some cases, asthma, which has been linked to muscle spasms.

Bridging an emotional gulf

Since boys have a greater tendency to lack verbal acumen, they are more likely to give vent to anger, fear and shame through movement and action. It is significant that the root of the word 'emotion' comes from *motere* – Latin for 'to move' – which, with its prefix *e-*, means 'to move away', because when boys find difficulty in expressing themselves verbally they tend to act out their emotions physically. While such an aggressive response is often interpreted by teachers as wilful malevolence, it is more likely to be a cry for help.

Many boys are offered little compensation at home, as there is often an emotional gulf separating them from their father, who may be absent, held in awe or simply unable to engage in meaningful communication. While boys yearn for a father to help them develop an emotional angle on life, in an effort to help them break free of their mother's attachment, on the path to becoming a man and a caring husband and father, the typical father–son relationship often leans towards competition, control and criticism.

Less theory and more real-life experiences, through practical application in Personal, Social and Health Education (PSHE) lessons in school, could do much to help develop a boy's emotional response towards the role of husband and father – e.g. if a boy was offered hands-on experience of holding, feeding and changing a real baby, it might make him a lot more cautious about unprotected sex and help him to develop more protective instincts toward women and more awareness about the possibility of pregnancy.

71

While there are obvious differences between boys and girls which need to be recognised and celebrated, such as unique hormonal influences and distinctive growth patterns in the brain's development, there seems to be too much distinction between the traits of what it is to be female – soft, vulnerable and dependent – and what it is to be male – strong, resilient and independent. By bridging this big divide, boys and girls could, at least, begin to meet as equals and, hopefully, be afforded the same opportunities. This can best be achieved by offering boys the same early emotional competence in handling their feelings as girls. Boys would then be far less likely to sabotage their education and personal lives.

A greater male presence in the classroom

The fact that most primary schools are dominated by a female staff can further alienate boys from the early learning experience. The latest government figures show that only 4,300 of the 215,000 early years teachers are men. It is perfectly possible for a boy never to set eyes on a man throughout his school day. Often boys, feeling outnumbered and overwhelmed by females, are desperate for good male role models, not only on the sports field, but also to provide guidance during their primary school years, particularly those without a father living at home. While women might once have been traditionally viewed as the more nurturing sex and regarded as better suited to teaching primary school children, which might have developed from a time when educated women were not allowed to seek employment in the outside world and took positions as governesses within the 'safe' confines of other people's homes, it's now time to redress the balance so that children learn about the world from a wider perspective.

The importance of physical activity

Boys and girls alike find it extremely difficult to be deskbound for long periods of time and need a lengthy timetabled period of physical activity every day as well as an environment that allows them more freedom to be physically active. If we are to accept that an adult's attention span is twenty minutes, we cannot expect any more from our children. By providing pupils with daily physical activity and exertion in addition to their break times, they would be less likely to be actively disruptive in the classroom and far more willing, and able, to give of their best in a lesson which demanded mental activity. If children do not have the opportunity to oxygenate their brains, they will slow down and underfunction. In the same way, if children do not exercise their bodies, we face a future nation of couch potatoes, with all the disease that entails.

A recent survey in *Sport England* reported that children are now spending less time on physical education than ever before. Only 11% of children aged 6–8 spent 2 or more hours a week in PE last year. The study also revealed that only 20% of pupils aged 9–11 now have 2 or more hours of PE a week, as opposed to nearly half in 1994. And yet PE is often the subject that teachers will forsake if they are under pressure or faced with inclement weather conditions. It can also be a subject that is withdrawn from children as a form of punishment. While it would be deemed unlawful for a child to miss English or Maths, PE, which is just as vital to the curriculum, if not more so because of its scarcity, is used as a carrot. No child should be made to miss any lesson, because they are all equally important.

Fitting the punishment to the crime

All forms of punishment have to be very carefully considered – e.g. detention, which is regarded by many pupils as the ultimate form of punishment, bar exclusion, is often given to a child who has merely expressed their emotions. Surely such punishment would be more suited to misdemeanours which impact others, such as hitting another child or damaging their property, forms of misbehaviour which are universally acknowledged to be wrong by all the members of a class. Emotional responses, which are usually peculiar to an individual and relate only to the child expressing them, need to be handled quite differently. If a child sees that they are punished for expressing their feelings, they will clam up and stop accessing them.

Leaving Mum

Children are at their most emotionally vulnerable when they leave the security of their home and mother to start school. At this time, mothers often feel that, while they brought their children up as lambs, they are now throwing them to the lions. School can feel very much like a jungle for infants, who find themselves in an alien environment in the company of children and adults they have never met before. Just how well received and welcomed they are into their new world is vitally important to their future response to education. They have to assimilate their home life into their school life, and vice versa, which can all be very confusing and unsettling. Instead of being able to learn in natural surroundings which use sensory experience, young children suddenly find themselves in the confines of classrooms, using books and technology

Infants look for the kind of individual attention and

recognition that they got from their mothers, but they soon learn that the role of the teacher is to bridge the gap between the child's home life and the world at large. As well as being introduced to academic skills, a reception child starts to become a social animal and learn cooperation and interdependency. As children enter a world of new and strange sensations, they also start to develop their feelings and emotions within a larger, and sometimes threatening, social framework.

On entering formal education, they are grouped according to their age as opposed to their maturity. If a school takes 'rising fives', three groups of children enter the class at three different times. This means that some summer-born children can be as much as eleven months younger than other children in the same class. In reception, this represents a fifth of their lives. This can distinctly disadvantage them at the outset and impact the rest of their school days – academically, physically and emotionally. An immature child can feel like a fish out of water simply because they're in the wrong class at the wrong stage in their development. Quite often, they never catch up with the other members of their class and are forever disadvantaged by their birthday. Instead of being a day to celebrate, it can be a day that determines how a child fits into the education system. One advantage of a school that takes pupils at four-plus is that all children can start school if they're four before September 1 and get a full year, which seems much fairer.

The rat race begins

Once a child starts school, there is a growing trend for parents to see learning as a race, a competition that must be won at all costs. Of course, such parents are only following the directive of overzealous education policymakers, who are forcing formalism on children at an ever younger age. But there are many children who would actually benefit from slowing down and starting formal education later rather than sooner. For instance, it has often been suggested that, since boys' fine-motor and cognitive skills generally develop less rapidly than girls', they would do better by starting school a year later and moving through the system a year after girls of the same chronological age. This option might also benefit some girls.

There is no doubt that when children do start school, they arrive with varying degrees of maturity, both chronological and emotional, as well as specific areas of intelligence. Arguably, the greatest challenge that education faces is that every child thinks and, therefore, learns differently. In addition, each child feels and emotes in a unique way. This makes it virtually impossible for a teacher, who is having to deal with 30-plus children, to recognise and nurture every child's individual needs. While an optimum class size of 30 is the aim of the government, a target of 20 would offer an environment in which a teacher might realistically help every child.

Full-time classroom assistance is not often in place, but it is vital in meeting the wide range of abilities and needs of young children. Pupils can gain considerable emotional benefits from a classroom assistant, especially one who is also a parent and who can offer a nurturing dimension to their school day. The teacher can also gain from having an adult assistant in the classroom, especially one with a sense of humour. The opportunity to share the vicissitudes of classroom life tends to put things into perspective and alleviate some of the pressure. An overburdened teacher will inevitably take their stress out on the children, thus greatly diminishing their capacity to enjoy the learning experience.

Teachers under stress

A recent report from The Teacher Support Line, the information, support and counselling helpline for teachers,
estimated that nearly half the country's teachers suffer from
stress, which can put them in a vulnerable position. The
service received 17,000 calls from the time it was set up in
September 1999 to February 2001, a period of less than 18
months.

The fact that there is a 50% rise in the number of teachers
questioned by police about alleged assaults (usually involving
a slap or a pull) may, in part, be due to our growing litigious
culture, where some parents take the law into their own
hands and report incidents directly to the police, but it is
also an indication that some teachers are at the end of their
emotional tether.

There is no doubt that the teaching profession attracts an
overabundance of idealistic and altruistic people who entered
the profession with the genuine aim of making a difference
to children's lives. Teachers have to be exceptional people
because they need a combination of effective technical,
organisational and interpersonal skills. But however special
they are, they are also human beings often stretched to
breaking point. When they had greater autonomy and were
given the opportunity to teach through their personalities
and curriculum strengths they seemed to be a lot happier
and less stressed. The current levels of anxiety and depression
amongst teachers seem to be triggered by a feeling of
purposelessness within the profession. This could well be
connected with the repetitive and laborious task of having
to deliver the National Curriculum.

Any type of institutional life can lead people to institutional
depression, but teachers seem to be particularly susceptible
right now, especially when faced with an Ofsted inspection.
The pressure that goes with the preparation and performance

for a visit by HMI, which is regarded by most teachers as 'an ordeal', can make the difference between a teacher who is able to cope and one who is driven over the edge. Some schools on special measures can even be subjected to termly inspections. It is a sad fact that some teachers have devoted their whole lives to teaching and can see no existence outside it! Their dedication is admirable but their institutionalised entrapment speaks volumes for teachers and children alike. Unlike in the times of the Inquisition, teachers are no longer burned at the stake, but they are being 'burned out' and their careers are constantly at stake, sometimes their very lives.

There have been several recent tragic cases of teachers who could see no way out of their professional crisis. In February 2001, a 45-year-old assistant headteacher at a school in Lewisham, South London, was found hanging in a minibus garage in the grounds of Sedgehill Comprehensive. The father of four, who taught vocational studies, outdoor pursuits and life skills, had been awarded the MBE for services to education in the previous year. In the autumn of 1999, a 33-year-old Cheshire teacher, fearing a negative inspector's report, hung herself before the inspection.

At Christmas 1999, a primary school teacher in Cambridgeshire wrote, 'I am now finding the stress of my job too much. The pace of work and the long days are more than I can do. I would like my ashes to be scattered in the woods...' Shortly after penning this note, she committed suicide by drowning herself in the River Ouse. More recently, in March 2000 a Birmingham teacher left a suicide note stating, 'My best is not good enough!'

While these cases are isolated and extreme, there are thousands of teachers who are suffering in stoical silence. The role of the teacher is now so demanding, multifaceted and under constant scrutiny that individuals can often feel overwhelmed and disillusioned by their chosen vocation.

Primary school teachers, who are rarely afforded the luxury of non-contact time, can go through the entire teaching day without a break if they happen to be on break duty, too. The amount of red tape and bureaucracy has become soul-destroying, and as a result teachers are beginning to feel cut off from the job they chose to do. It is hardly surprising that the profession is threatening a mass exodus and that 50% of the present workforce is expected to leave over the next ten years. Of course, all this negative energy has a knock-on effect for pupils.

Grouping and setting

One of the long-term grievances and most challenging parts of a teacher's job is the nonsensical ratio of children to teacher. The only way teachers can cope is to subdivide the class according to their assessment of the children's ability. This may be a great organisational tool for the teacher, but it can cause untold damage to a child's self-esteem. No matter how hard a teacher tries to disguise the names of the groupings, children soon work out the real truth of their position within the class.

As we know from people who failed the 11-plus, which was specifically designed to assess a child's intelligence quotient, the assessment and grading system can be spiritually wounding and make a child feel defective before they've barely had an opportunity to prove themselves. Children need to feel that they are just as important as everyone else, but grouping and setting does quite the opposite. It cuts deep into a child's psyche and causes rifts in the dynamics of a class as one group cuts off from another.

As pupils assimilate their teacher's view of them, the self-fulfilling prophecy comes into play and children start to perform according to their teacher's expectation. Children can secretly anguish over what's seen as a vote of no confidence in them and either perform at a consistently low level or give up trying entirely. They start to label themselves in derogatory terms such as 'rubbish', 'hopeless' and 'thick' in relation to a particular subject, and it is then very hard to reverse this self-image. It can limit them for their entire education and beyond.

Children at the top end of ability groupings tend to be those who can cope in conformist mode without the aid of the teacher. It is not uncommon to see gifted children, often deep thinkers, assigned to a lower ability group incompatible with their real ability simply because they are nonconformists and exhibit erratic performance. Very often they are actually bored and browbeaten by the system and rebel by deliberate underachievement and indolence. It is only when they are presented with a stimulating task which challenges their intelligence that they excel.

Gifted children

Gifted children often exhibit disruptive, demanding and difficult behaviour in class. They can be eccentric, immature, argumentative and contradictory, which can make them unpopular with teachers and children. They can also be negatively labelled as fidgety, attention-seeking, dreamy and distant. They tend to switch off because they are not being switched on. Again, the whole of their school lives can be unfulfilled because their giftedness goes unrecognised and unsupported. While their presence can put extra pressure on teachers and sometimes make them feel irritated, they are as capable as their peers of producing pearls.

High ability does not always show itself in test results or high attainment. Some exceptionally gifted children are often reluctant to manifest their talents in a classroom setting. They often prefer to be liked and accepted by their classmates

80

rather than admired by their teachers. At the moment, there is very little provision for the approximately 10% of children with special abilities such as a musical or artistic talent. We now know that children have the capacity for multiple intelligences, and yet a heightened aesthetic or sensual intelligence often goes unrecognised or undervalued.

Children with learning difficulties

Then there is a large percentage of children with learning problems. While 15–20% of children require special help for learning difficulties, no more than 2% of these children are placed in recognised special classes or schools. Some suffer in silence for years. I knew a 16-year-old boy who was a school refuser, but the reason behind his non-attendance went unnoticed for most of his school life. Outwardly he projected an able and intelligent persona and was very popular with his peers. He exhibited talent in the arts but showed no academic interest or aptitude. It was not until he accepted a leading role in a school musical that his underlying problem became apparent.

While still refusing school during the day, he never missed an after-school rehearsal for the musical. It was evident that he had a high degree of sensual intelligence which did not equate with his low academic performance. It was only when I asked him to write down a few notes that I began to see a problem. He showed a determined resistance to the task which was completely out of character. A few weeks later, he was diagnosed as dyslexic, a problem which had blighted his entire school life. Fortunately, he is now receiving one-to-one help for his learning difficulty, whilst undertaking a performing arts diploma at college. He was one of the lucky ones. There are thousands of children who suffer in silence and never get the help they need to fulfil their potential.

Children suffering in silence

Nearly every child operates a 'code of silence' in one or more aspects of their life. The most obvious is a child who falls prey to sexual abuse. The predators cleverly gain the trust of their victims and bribe or threaten them with all sorts of repercussions if they share their little 'secret! It seems to be part of a child's make-up to keep secrets rather than be labelled a 'telltale', a 'snitch' or a 'rat'. They are, of course, often threatened with reprisals.

So few children have the confidence or capability to defend themselves or others. I am convinced that this is because they have been so repressed and intimidated by their parents and teachers that they have very little faith or trust in their adult carers to protect or defend them. They feel that whatever they have to say will probably fall on deaf ears or will not be believed. This is a very serious form of betrayal and needs our urgent attention.

I believe one of the reasons children are so vulnerable is that they are invariably raised to feel inferior to adults and are forced to obey them whatever their commands and demands. Hence a victim mentality is already set up in children by their parents and teachers – obey or else!

Bullying at school

We all know that classrooms are full of sarcasm, teasing and bantering at someone else's expense. Since it is an accepted mode of communication, most of it is shrugged off as inconsequential. But there are occasions when constant taunting develops into bullying. If it is not nipped in the bud, it can lead to victims underachieving academically, playing truant from school, running away from home, depression, eating disorders, self-mutilation and even suicide.

The problem is that bullying is not always taken seriously. Instead of acknowledging it as a totally unacceptable form of behaviour, many adults, including some teachers, argue that it is part of human nature and that kids have to learn to deal with it as part of growing up. It is certainly true that mild forms of bullying, verbal taunts such as 'div', 'spaz', 'slag' and 'geek', are almost endemic to our society. While none of it could be categorised as a criminal offence, the fact that it involves the use of aggression with the intent of hurting another person, it has to be regarded as criminal behaviour.

Bullying occurs in every type of school and in every age group. No class, culture, creed or age is exempt. Girls are just as capable of bullying as boys. In fact, there is an increase in the number of aggressive girls who are bullying and intimidating boys with lewd comments and sexual gestures. Bullying, which always involves an imbalance of power between the bully and the victim, takes three broad forms: physical, verbal and emotional. A fourth form, that takes on a 'menacing' perspective involving demands of the victim by the bully, is less common.

In my experience, bullying is a symptom of mental or emotional distress on the part of the bully, a cry for help. By attacking someone who is vulnerable, the bully is expressing and projecting their own feelings of vulnerability and insecurity. It is a coping mechanism. By bullying others the bully is denying and protecting their own sensitivity and their own sense of dereliction and helplessness.

There seem to be several common characteristics that produce and typify bullies, most of which stem from the structure and relationships of the family unit rather than social or economic considerations. Bullies are often bullied themselves at home and raised in a family which condones violence and bullying. Their parents are either overly strict or lax in the area of discipline The children are ignored or tyrannised at home and are not allowed to express their feelings and emotions adequately. They often feel inadequate to cope with everyday tasks. They have a desire to pass on their pain and humiliation.

Bullies are invariably low achievers at school. They are often children who enjoy being in charge and control of a gang. They can be overly-confident, obnoxious and used to getting their own way or, conversely, have no sense of self-worth. Their bullying can be prolonged or triggered by a particular incident such as the birth of a baby, a family tragedy or a distressing event in their own life. They are often quite unconscious of the pain they are inflicting and can be motivated by peer pressure. They tend to believe that bullying is preferable to being bullied and often operate in a covert way behind a mask of anonymity.

Bullies' targets are often children who are a bit different – an obese or small child, someone who wears glasses or a hearing aid, someone who has a problem with personal hygiene – or, alternatively, a figure of envy – a boffin, a teacher's pet, a child who comes from a stable background or a well-off family, someone with good looks or a particular talent. Also being targeted are minority groups having to deal with racist and homophobic bullying.

Most victims are sensitive, gentle children who have good relationships with their parents, particularly boys who are closely-bonded to their mothers, and too nice to fight back. Often described as 'softies', they cannot understand why they should be a target. Persistent bullying can lead to long-term problems for the victims such as an inability to trust people and a feeling of worthlessness. Much like victims of sexual abuse, they can feel that in some way they deserve to be abused and that they are entirely responsible for what has happened.

Other types of victim can be children who actually enjoy the attention bullying can engender, albeit negative. Such children can have similar problems to the bullies, and they feed off each other's pain and anguish. In fact, some children switch from being victims to bullies. Bullying not only harms the bullies and the victims. Bystanders (witnesses) can also be implicated when they fail to report an incident. Bullying at school would be much easier to deal with if the onlookers had the courage to report bullies as soon as they started their taunts. A code of silence can lead to feelings of guilt about not intervening, anxiety because they might be the next victims and powerlessness, somewhat akin to survivor's guilt.

Much can be done by parents to empower bullied children. Since the emotions are always evident in the interplay between the bully and the victim it is important to establish how the victim is feeling about being victimised. Negative feelings projected by bullies could well mirror the victimisation and judgement felt by victims from their parents. Above all, children need to know that they are loved unconditionally by their parents and not feel that they need to change to be loved. It is not enough for parents to want their children to be less fearful and vulnerable to bullies. Parents need to be more assertive in their own behaviour, to make changes in themselves to become happier and more positive people, and then mirror these qualities for their children. This encourages children to respond differently to vulnerable and fearful situations. It is then perfectly possible for victims of bullying to convert their feelings of anger, anxiety and helplessness into self-esteem, power and detachment. This kind of transformation turns victims into victors and bullies retreating to find other targets.

A bullying heritage

In looking at the problem of bullying in our schools, we have to bear in mind that Britain has a history of institutionalised bullying which was nurtured in our public schools. Not only have we allowed hundreds of children, including members of our Royal Family, to be sent away from the care of their parents to fend for themselves emotionally, we have also subjected them to sadistic physical abuse such as flogging and all kinds of initiation rites. Past traditions include being tossed in a blanket to the ceiling at Eton, hands being seared with burning wood at Winchester and pupils being forced to drink a jug of muddy water, strongly doused with salt, at Rugby.

During his days at an orphan's school at the end of the nineteenth century, Charlie Chaplin recalled vivid memories of the punishment that took place every Friday:

> 'On the right and in front of the desk was an easel with wrist straps dangling and from the frame a birch hung ominously... Captain Hindrum, a retired naval man weighing about 200 pounds, stood poised, measuring [the cane] across the boy's buttocks. Then he would lift it high and with a swish bring it down across the boy's bottom. The spectacle was terrifying and invariably a boy fell out of rank in a faint... If a culprit received more than three strokes, his cries were appalling. The strokes were paralysing, so that the victim had to be carried to one side.'

Describing punishments at his school between the wars, Roald Dahl recalled, '[The Headmaster] used to deliver the most vicious beatings to boys under his care. At the end, a basin, a sponge and a small clean towel were produced by the head teacher, and the victim was told to wash away the blood before pulling up his trousers.'

A high proportion of our society still condones corporal punishment as a viable deterrent in our schools. As recently as 1983, the TV Times conducted an opinion poll asking three sectors of the population, 'Do you approve of corporal punishment?' The results showed that 62% of pupils, 81% of parents and 54% of teachers were in favour of corporal punishment. While corporal punishment is no longer used in most schools, it is worth considering how the obvious sado-masochistic streak that lies within so many people who are responsible for the care of children, and in some of the children themselves, is now being channelled.

Reversing the bullying cycle

There is no doubt that the majority of children in today's society frequently witness teachers and parents in bullying mode, using shouting, sarcasm, intimidation and physical restraint to keep children under control. In addition, children see powerful role models of aggressive behaviour in films, on television, in comics and amongst their sporting heroes. These models emphasise the negative values of physical prowess, bad language and aggressive heroes – both male and female – who defeat their enemies by violent means. Bullies are merely following the behaviour patterns they observe in their daily lives where the strong trample and triumph over the weak.

Unless their behaviour is checked at school, young bullies will grow up to be big bullies and wreak havoc out in the world, at work and at home. Some will be unable to hold down a job or maintain a relationship and will end up in trouble with the law because they tend to think they're above it. Should they have children of their own, they are likely to perpetuate the bullying cycle.

It is the responsibility of each school to alleviate the problem by facing the issue as a united staff and to adopt a caring ethos of being 'a telling school'. Teachers need to promote and instil in their pupils an anti-bullying policy which nurtures values such as tolerance and respect for each other. INSET days on strategies for coping with bullying would help teachers, and specific PSHE lessons and circle times on bullying would provide the emotional support pupils need to deal with a problem that must no longer be swept under the carpet.

As a nation we take pride in the belief that the principles of our education system are fundamentally sound, even though they may be seriously flawed. Accepting that life's unfair, most adults take the view that if they had to suffer the indignities of the education system then their children can, too. But it's that same kind of resigned and defeatist attitude that allows most people to go on living in various states of fear and insecurity. Fortunately, there are courageous souls who are not afraid of wanting a bit more for their children and would like to find an antidote to the poisonous pedagogy that has plagued our society for generations.

Chapter Three

A Future for Education

A complete transformation

We are constantly hearing that it's time to stop reforming schools and start improving them. But education has already seen more reforms and improvements than any other government department over the past forty years. What education needs is a complete transformation in emphasis. Although there is a resistance to change because it might cause instability or collapse, we desperately need to move away from the notion that education and teaching are industrial processes that have to be imposed on pupils and realise that children learn not by what they're told about something but how they feel about it. Learning should not be a painful process of indoctrination but a joyful process of exploration. Children are not mules to be kick-started and force-fed. They function best when they are relaxed and receptive. At present, our education system is based on a teacher imparting facts and figures and then trying to ascertain what a child can remember and, hopefully, understand. What we need is a situation where children have the free will to absorb what they want to from the environment and the creative freedom to develop it.

One of my greatest concerns is that we're pushing children so hard in the wrong direction that we could see an even greater toll on their physical and mental health. Children experience great difficulty trying to reconcile their own expectations with those of their teachers, which is part of a wider problem concerning the way children and adults relate to each other. Teachers need to help children feel far more accepted and acceptable as individuals within school and society. This is why it is vitally important for teachers to be humanists and artists as well as scientists and analysts.

If we think about it, children's earliest responses to the world are basically on a sensual and instinctual level. The fact that children are sentient beings before they can reason, reflect or judge is very telling in terms of what makes them feel secure and loved.

What we ask children to do at school is to operate mainly on an intellectual, conscious level that is simplistic and capable of processing only one decision at a time, instead of an instinctual, unconscious level that is multifaceted and capable of a range of decisions. By placing so much emphasis on intellectual endeavour, we are impeding children's progress by offering them only a partial interpretation of the world and its workings.

When children look for answers about the eternal laws of the universe, they do not want a lopsided or one-sided point of view. When children ask who created the world and where you go to when you die, they are seeking a well-rounded answer that will satisfy their spirit and soul as well as their intellect. For this to happen, a teacher needs to create an atmosphere of exploration, of lateral thinking, of endless possibilities. It's not the role of the teacher to come up with a definitive answer, or alter children's existing beliefs, but to present them with as many sides of an argument as possible and let them make up their own minds.

Adults listening to children

In the role of enabler and facilitator, teachers need to ensure that they make time to actively listen to every child on a one-to-one basis at least once a week. This is vitally important because in the daily course of their school life, a child in a class of 30+ is constantly being interrupted, spoken at, answered with an inappropriate response and under pressure to get their point of view across before the teacher's attention is taken by another pupil. In many instances, the teacher can actually block the flow of what pupils want to say. It is vitally important that children have the undivided attention of their teacher so as to share their thoughts and feelings without interruptions, questions or judgements. By actively listening, teachers are showing children they are interested in their well-being, which helps them to analyse and reflect their concerns. They are then empowered to come up with a resolution.

Children listening to each other

Children also need to be nurtured in the art of listening to each other. One of the best ways this can be done is through circle time. Breaking with the traditional barrier of sitting at desks, sitting in the round allows direct eye contact and a more intimate opportunity for pupils to hear, talk about and share feelings with their peers. This experience also encourages greater equality and a sense of being valued that is conducive to sharing feelings and expressing opinions without fear of interruption or put-down.

The same sort of skills can be nurtured by using the technique of brainstorming. This can also be done in a circle and is useful in gathering ideas and encouraging creativity as well as nurturing the concept of teamwork.

Everyone is equal and has an opportunity to be heard without the pressure of evaluation or judgement.

Debating is another powerful source for nurturing listening skills as well as self-expression. It enables children to state their opinions, argue a position, explore feelings, listen to other points of view, make a decision for or against a contentious issue, but still remain respectful of the opposition. Here, pupils have an opportunity to see the teacher in the role of neutral onlooker, a listener who is not asked to agree or disagree, offer an opinion or make a judgement.

Co-creation in the classroom

While children look to their teachers as the source of inspiration and stimulation, pupils must then be given the opportunity to launch their own original ideas. In this way, teachers and children become co-creators, which satisfies both parties. The concept of co-creation is nothing new and was greatly valued by Socrates (c. 400 BC), who said, 'I shall only ask him and not teach him, and he shall share the enquiry with me and do you watch and see if you find me telling or explaining anything to him, instead of eliciting his opinion.'

Co-creation is the absolute opposite of the 'them and us' approach to teaching which children have always resented. Some teachers find it difficult to relinquish the power that goes with ruling a classroom and can be quite protective of their kingdom and its subjects. At the root of their power struggle can be a desire for revenge for the power that was exerted over them by their teachers. It is this kind of imperialism that works against the principle of co-creation.

Everywhere we go in schools there are messages of how teachers regard their pupils. Children are often faced with blatant signs of inequality when confronted with physical signs such as 'Staff Only', 'No students beyond this point' and 'Strictly no access'. Even though they know some of them pertain to safety precautions, forbidding signs like these work against the idea of inclusion.

In the classroom environment, pupils are further subjected to segregation by their peers' achievements and their teachers' view of them. Star charts, house points, exam results, ability groupings, pupil of the week and gender stereotyping all work against equality. It seems to take a dramatic event before teachers and pupils are reminded that they are, in fact, working towards a goal of mutual respect and understanding.

A few years ago, I can recall a student commenting on the death of a 16-year-old boy who had been brutally stabbed to death one Friday night, just hours after scoring four goals for the school football team. 'It's at times like these that you realise we're not so very different. The headteacher, the teachers, the parents and the pupils may have different roles within the school and the community, but we all feel the same. Our grief is one grief, our pain is one pain!'

Children as decision makers

Teachers need to have a greater appreciation that education is a two-way thing, that children can teach them as much as they can teach the children. This reciprocity needs to be the cornerstone of school life, where each individual is encouraged to contribute as well as benefit, where both teacher and student stand to gain. As Wordsworth said, 'The child is father of the man', and if children aren't encouraged to be part of the launch of a creation, they will lose interest and feel manipulated by the teacher. A cooperative approach to teaching encourages children to believe, and grow to know, that they are the absolute creators of their own experience. This is why work experience and voluntary work for disaffected year 10s is so invaluable. By working with others and being of value to the community, they not only have an opportunity to develop their individual self-worth, but also to nurture co-creative skills which will stand them in good stead for the rest of their lives.

Wherever possible, rather than having facts and figures imposed on them, pupils need to be empowered as creators and decision makers of their own projects. They need more opportunities for learning through active self-discovery and less accent on memory and rote. Young people thrive on choices and need to play a more active role in helping to plan the curriculum.

A universe of their own

Adults can start by acknowledging that young children already have their own quite sophisticated society, which is largely separate from the adult world. It is a universe of rituals and songs which start to manifest themselves in the playground. It includes nursery rhymes such as 'Rain, Rain Go Away' and 'Eeny, Meeny, Miney Mo' and chants such as 'London Bridge Is Falling Down' and 'The Grand Old Duke of York', which have been reverentially passed down from generation to generation.

These are not taught by parents or teachers. They belong exclusively to the world of children, who teach each other the words and tunes. It's a world that needs and deserves respect from adults. It's little wonder that many children describe play time as the best part of the day, not only because it represents freedom from the quiet and sedentary structure of the classroom, an environment where social expression is usually nipped in the bud, but because it's an experience relatively free from adult intervention, an opportunity to skip, swing, run and jump without restraint.

Play time not only enables children to develop their sensory, motor and social skills, it's also an opportunity to nurture their emotions and imagination. While my son would be perfectly happy to miss his formal lessons, there is nothing worse for him than to miss his play time. To be 'benched' for the duration of his break is tantamount to imprisonment, because play represents liberty. As Tim Gill, director of the Children's Play Council, says, 'School playgrounds may look like chaotic places, but play time is one of the few oases in children's lives where they can be themselves.'

Playground interaction is an amazingly powerful source for observing how much we underestimate children's innate intelligence. It highlights their ability to work things out for themselves and focuses on their powerful intuitive skills for accessing the adult world. Although they have never experienced milestones such as giving birth, death and parenthood, they can act out these events with a sophistication far beyond their chronological age. How else could an infant lay down and die and the next minute stand up and return to life so victoriously without some precognitive notion of resurrection?

The imposition of formal education

Although pre-school children are capable of using universal symbolisation like this, infants seem to become a lot more self-conscious once they start formal education. We have to ask ourselves whether this is because children feel crushed by their every move being led by the teacher. At school they are no longer the masters of their own destinies but the slaves of their teacher's will. Many children are so anxious to please the teacher and to meet the criteria of what is considered appropriate to fit into the system at school that they stop thinking for themselves. They give up their natural and powerful way of thinking and adopt a false and far less effective method. They start to clam up when asked to do anything new or challenging.

There are only a few children who become good at thinking according to the expectations of the school. Most are intimidated, fearful and discouraged, while some stop thinking altogether. In many instances, school is a place where pupils have a low opinion of themselves as learners, which sets them on a road to becoming underachieving human beings with low self-worth and an inability to think for themselves. As songwriter Paul Simon sang in an eighties postscript, 'When I look back on all the crap I learned in high school, it's a wonder I can think at all.'

The only way we can reverse this is for schools to stop making judgements according to their own yardsticks and to try and present children with pleasurable and meaningful experiences according to their needs. So much of what is taught today is meaningless to children because it is fragmented, isolated and dissociated from anything else. Learning experiences need to be contextualised not just for the development of the mind alone, but also for the body, the feelings and the imagination.

This is why children gain so much from outward-bound and camping expeditions, where they are in touch with nature, offered the opportunity to fend for themselves and learn meaningful life skills. They can learn more about themselves and their place within society from a weekend field trip than in an entire academic year in a classroom. Learning by active experience is by far the most effective method because it gives young people a feeling of owning their own learning. This takes a lot of pressure off the teacher and helps students to become more independent and responsible.

Adults tend to judge children purely on their outer manifestations and to disregard their private and inner worlds. This is a realm filled with anxieties and doubts as well as dreams and fantasies. Children are more likely to share their innermost feelings and emotions through creative activities such as poetry, art, music, drama, dance and film. We often regard their artistic expression as haphazard, accidental and of the moment, but their imaginative output is usually much more symbolic and meaningful than that. It often stems from a memory or opinion that they want to relive or express which cannot always be put into words. It might represent any of their emotions, such as joy, fear, anger or resentment. In this way, the arts can help a child to clarify a past, present or future concern or experience.

Aesthetic knowledge

An education which does not include a strong aesthetic dimension is failing to cultivate and develop a child's feelings and emotions. The only way this can happen is if all teachers are encouraged to nurture their own feelings and emotions and have the resources to impart knowledge that goes beyond the delivery of facts and figures.

Since children are natural trailblazers who prefer to seek out new and uncharted territory rather than tried and tested paths, teachers need to be imbued with an absolute belief that aesthetic knowledge is just as important as intellectual knowledge. While aestheticism cannot be logically quantified, it nurtures the senses and imagination and helps children to know and understand the world at large.

From the time of the Greek philosopher Plato the role of aesthetics in education has been considered but never fully integrated. In equating education with 'true knowledge' rather than 'opinion', Plato divided his ideal society into the ruling class, the 'guardians', and the working class, the 'artisans'. The guardians had an education which gave them an intrinsic 'true knowledge', things that were valuable in themselves such as art and music, while the artisans acquired extrinsic skills which equipped them for a particular job, such as arithmetic for the accountant or woodwork for the carpenter.

As part of their birthright, children are natural aesthetes, but their aesthetic potential cannot be fully realised unless it is nurtured and developed through the arts. As states rise and fall and traditional religions disappear or change their original doctrines and become less relevant in many people's lives (only about 7% of the population go to church on a Sunday), it could be argued that the arts are needed more than ever to help give significance and spiritual meaning to a child's life. And yet it is well known that the National Curriculum has marginalised artistic and creative subjects in favour of science and technology. While art and music are included in the core curriculum, drama, dance and film are subsumed into wider subject categories. This is probably because the arts are often considered non-vocational, woolly and vague 'frills', a form of entertainment and leisure, while the sciences are seen as vocational and having purpose and conviction. The truth is that the arts cannot be quantified, while the sciences can.

But children need to be encouraged to appreciate things not just for the knowledge they can acquire but for the effect they can have on their feelings. They need to be open to experiences which transport them from the mundane towards something infinite which has communal significance.

The advent of the computer age has certainly helped children to access information and make their lives more efficient and streamlined, but as John Mortimer commented in a leader in the *Daily Mail* in February 2001: 'No computer has been used to write better plays than Shakespeare's or

Chekhov's, wiser arguments than those of Socrates, or funnier books than P.G. Wodehouse... Education should help fill your mind with stories and scraps of poetry and music and pictures which will be a pleasure and a consolation throughout your life.'

Alternative methods of education

Teachers are often resistant to an aesthetic approach to teaching, either because they are uncertain of how to go about it, or because they are uncertain of the benefits within the context of the contemporary world. It is this same scepticism that makes many parents and educational psychologists reject alternative methods of education such as Steiner and Montessori, which give ample scope to the artistic and aesthetic potential of a child, because they argue they are incompatible with the real world.

They feel that they do not prepare children for the competitive work ethic of the commercial marketplace. That mode of thinking is fine for those who have no desire to improve the education system or the world. But it is only by transforming our education system, so that children fulfil their intellectual and imaginative potential, that the world will change for the better. The state of the education system and the state of the world are one and the same thing – as one prospers so does the other.

The Steiner philosophy

The Steiner philosophy places a great deal of emphasis on nurturing children's feelings and emotions through an arts-based approach which embraces a connection between nature and spirit. It believes that art as a form of knowledge is equal to science and that the two disciplines need to be unified, and also that when children are allowed to express themselves artistically and in a way that interests them their ability to concentrate takes on a new dimension. With no formal tests or exams, no sitting in rows or learning how to read or write until the age of seven, Steiner pupils spend their day singing, drawing, painting and dancing as well as farming and harvesting corn and baking their own bread.

A Steiner teacher is expected to have a balanced view of life and education – an intellectual–sensual side and a moral–spiritual side. The Steiner approach to teacher training is free of rules, concepts and formal doctrines favouring a flexible and creative approach towards knowledge which incorporates a spiritual and emotional dimension as well as a scientific and analytical one.

One of the most dynamic elements of a Steiner curriculum is eurythmy, which is adapted from the ancient spirit of Greek dance. It is used in Steiner schools, not only as an art form but also a means of healing and education. Fairy tales, myths and legends, which existed long before logic and mathematics, are also widely used to conjure up imaginative images and express higher truths. This kind of experience is believed to encourage contemplation and reflection and can nurture significant metaphysical insights.

The Montessori method

The Montessori method, originally designed for nursery and infant education, relies on auto-education 'by means of liberty in a prepared environment' and stresses the importance of a child's senses and the training of those senses. One of its philosophies is that real education comes only when the intellect rises above and dominates the information it has received. The Montessori philosophy is based on the belief that all children are capable of being creative, have a desire to learn and need freedom to decide when and what they want to learn without imposition from a teacher. It relies on individual work and creative expression, with each member of a class rarely working on the same thing at the same time. Using materials such as beads arranged in number units for teaching arithmetic and small slabs of wood to help train the eye to move from left to right in preparation for reading, Montessori infants are allowed to work at their own pace whenever and for however long they wish. There is also a lot of emphasis on sensorial materials and tasks for practical life – preparing lunch, arranging flowers, setting the table and cleaning shoes.

Its founder, child psychologist Maria Montessori, believed that 'Little children, because of their innocence, can feel in a purer and more intense manner, even if less definitely than the adult, the need of God's presence. Their souls seem to be more open to divine intuitions than the adult's, in spite of the latter's more perfectly developed intelligence and skill in reasoning.' She also observed that a teacher needs to 'purge his soul of those two mortal sins to which teachers are particularly prone – pride and anger.'

While it is unlikely that every principle of the Steiner or Montessori methods will become mainstream, we would do well to take heed of their essence and, at least, work toward a balance between the sciences and the arts. While most of the curriculum is concerned with the here and now, the arts free children from the pressures of the moment and the stresses of the modern world. They can be a portal for unfolding hidden meanings about the past, the present and the future. They can also offer us metaphors to illuminate our human existence and better understand the human condition. Given their extraordinary ability to unlock a child's ability to learn, it is hard to believe that they could be so marginalised, often downgraded to extra-curricular status.

Integrating the arts

Children can be so deprived of the arts in the primary school curriculum that when they are offered music, dance or drama they regard them as 'treats' rather than subjects which are woven into the daily fabric of their school timetable. Primary school colleagues speak of the uncontainable excitement that children express when liberated from the literacy or numeracy hour and of how they are not quite sure how to behave away from a desk. But if the arts were properly and fully integrated into the curriculum, I'm sure children's behaviour in the classroom would be far less challenging overall.

Music

Children instinctively know that there is no better way to start the day than to share a song or hymn. The opportunity to vocalise together can be one of the great benefits of daily assembly. It not only brings children together for the common purpose of sharing thoughts and feelings, it also provides an opportunity for vocal expression and listening to music. Being stimulated by a piece of music as children file in and out of assembly can coordinate their intellects and emotions for the rest of the school day.

It's been proven that listening to classical music, such as a Mozart sonata, can have a remarkably soothing and focusing effect on pupils. But this device could be regularly used in all sorts of other ways, ranging from a source of inspiration for an art lesson to a stimulus for creative writing or an accompaniment to reciting tables or spellings. It could also be used for a set timed challenge, to create a change in atmosphere, a guided visualisation or to enhance a theme or topic, e.g. listening to the operettas of Gilbert and Sullivan as a prelude to discussing the Victorians. The rhythms of music are not only a vital resource in the music lesson itself, they can be useful in helping children to access hidden rhythms in other aspects of their lives.

In an article entitled 'Children Need Music', featured in *The Times* in November 1998, the late Lord Yehudi Menuhin, one of the world's greatest violinists, spoke of society looking on a child as 'an empty sack into which we stuff facts and knowledge.' He wrote, 'Art reflects the refinement of a civilisation. Violence and sex are all right, translated as energy and desire, but in their crude state are uncivilised. Music goes both ways. You make yourself heard and listen to others... Music draws upon feeling and thinking, joining the emotional with the rational. It brings out the best in a child or young adult.'

He also made the point that to include singing and dancing does not involve a lot of financial investment: 'Everyone has a voice, lungs, eyes and a heart with which to communicate. It comes from the inner life of a child... When they sing and dance they think better, understand better, are more communicative with each other and the world.'

It has been proven that music engages both sides of the brain. Norman Weinberger, Professor of Psychology at the University of Southern California, reported, 'Brain scans taken during musical performances show that virtually the entire cerebral cortex is active while musicians are playing.' Professors Shaw and Leng, also at the University of Southern California, undertook research with 74 college students which showed that performance in spatial–temporal reasoning tests, manipulation of shapes, understanding of symmetry, proportional reasoning and mental imagery, improved after students had listened to ten minutes of Mozart.

In another recent project involving 136 second-year pupils at an elementary school in one of Los Angeles' poorest neighbourhoods, Shaw found that pupils who read music and learned to play the piano showed increased competency in numeracy. 'The learning of music emphasises thinking in space and time. When children learn rhythm, they are learning ratios, fractions and proportions.' In 1993, when looking for a link between musical sound discrimination and reading ability, Lamb and Gregory found a 'high degree of correlation between how well children could read both standard and phonic reading material and how well they could discriminate pitch.'

Dance

While dance can obviously develop body awareness and aid coordination, it is greatly undervalued in its ability to deal with social issues, e.g. cooperation between boys and girls and the healing of gender issues. It is rich in cultural tradition and can help children to understand social behavioural patterns and contexts. It also raises self-esteem and self-awareness. Being free of conventional classroom practice, it can be an important form of escape from the mundane and can nurture improvisational skills.

Drama

Drama, too, is an invaluable multidimensional discipline with the potential to embrace all the arts. It allows collective activity and a sense of commitment, where children are working together on planning, researching, appraising and appreciating for a common purpose. It can be particularly useful for children who are alienated by the formal curriculum and who struggle with written English. It enhances group cooperation and encourages social skills. It develops empathy and an opportunity to understand other people's points of view. It also helps children to solve problems and form opinions as well as nurturing an appreciation of the values, issues and cultures of today's world.

Visual art

As for the benefits of the visual arts, it has been proven that children's personality traits manifest themselves in their works of art, e.g. colour can have a link with emotion; line and form is usually associated with energy and control; while space tells us something about how children feel about their environment, e.g. whether it is restricting or liberating. It can also reveal how children feel about their place within society and the universe, whether they feel a success or a failure, what they've gained from the past and want for the future.

The arts and emotional intelligence

In an article for the *Observer* in 1998, John MacBeath, in his capacity as Director of the Quality in Education Centre at the University of Strathclyde, spoke of the arts as being,

'if you wish to be historical, the most deeply rooted ways of knowing. Music does something profoundly important to the chemistry of left and right brain, and plays a major role in memory and emotional intelligence. Art, dance and drama can not only make for a more satisfying life but can be used directly to help develop those qualities so prized by employers – communication skills, self-confidence, self-presentation, problem solving, teamwork, independent thinking, breadth of interest, capacity for learning.'

A year before, Andrew Davies, screenwriter and former teacher/trainer, wrote an article for *The Times Educational Supplement* entitled 'Why Creativity Must Be Fostered', in which he observed, 'I'm not saying it's got to be all self-expression and poetry, brainstorming and discovery learning, but I am saying that these things are vitally important and if we don't cherish them we might as well pack it in.'

The arts are often at their most powerful when seen within the framework of an alliance, which is where my interest lies. When used in collaboration, they are capable of incredible transformations in children's self-belief and learning. From my own experience, the arts in harmony can help children to make decisions, accept responsibility, develop an awareness and sensitivity to others as well as nurture self-discipline and cooperative skills. They also help young people to manage their feelings, deal with stress, and build an awareness of their personal limitations and potential for growth.

Greek tragedy

My most vivid and rewarding experience of seeing the arts in collaboration was working on a simplified version of Sophocles' *Antigone*. The project involved fourteen pupils, four of them statemented, from a junior school fed by a densely populated working-class community which is now part of an Education Action Zone. On undertaking this Greek tragedy, which comes from one of the world's oldest forms of theatre, I was greeted with great scepticism from the teaching staff and parents. As the multidimensional project progressed – it included Greek masks and costumes, two original Greek dance sequences, three original songs plus a violin solo and a trumpet duet – there were certainly times when it seemed so daunting and overambitious I was tempted to give up and admit defeat.

106

But, even at my lowest ebb, something kept me going. It must have been the children's determined persistence with a project which was so obviously out of their normal experience and light years away from the pop culture of today. If they could keep going, so could I. I do not remember a rehearsal that was anything but chaotic and frustrating. Even the final dress rehearsal showed no promise of refinement and seemed devoid of shape or form.

But the very next day something extraordinary happened which was to change my perception of teaching forever. The children were invited to perform the play for a group of postgraduate student teachers at their university drama studio. I went along with my heart in my mouth, believing that the children were under-rehearsed and not ready to give a credible performance before an audience. How wrong I was.

From the commanding opening procession, with the dramatic effect of masks and headdresses fashioned from real flowers, to the poignant delivery of the Chorus to the ritualism of the Greek dance sequences and the tragic death of Antigone, it was a spine-chilling experience which touched every sense.

The mature students seemed riveted by the intensity of the children's interpretation, and some were even moved to tears. The young performers were given a standing ovation. I felt like a bystander who had merely presented the children with a script, a form and some direction. What the children did with it was nothing short of a miracle.

A few days later, I received a letter from one of the student teachers in the audience:

'It made me feel that there is beauty and joy in the world. Here was a group of children with little or no experience of the aesthetic getting an opportunity to express their feelings and raw emotions. To see them in this sort of place, doing this sort of thing, was unbelievable. They are so used to being transfixed to a television set and their lives, in general, are totally devoid of art. It is through this kind of experience that children grow to understand about the beauty of life and about their individual and communal place within society. For me, this incredible event was the equivalent of the day I discovered Wordsworth. If you can ignite one small spark, it's worth all the effort!'

Children's opera

While this experience would be difficult to surpass, I've witnessed other powerful examples of children's lives and perceptions changing forever through the arts. During a three-year term as director of music at a high school on special measures, I fostered close links with the Glyndebourne Opera House Education Department. Eleven pupils, ranging from twelve to sixteen years of age, all from working-class backgrounds, with little or no experience on their school stage let alone in a world-class opera house, were offered principal roles in the children's opera *Misper*. They were not only thrown in at the deep end, given their inexperience as performers, but they also had to perform and interact with middle-class cast members in a milieu known for its snobbery and elitism.

Gradually managing to transcend their social class, they also visibly grew in self-perception and a sense of possibility. This was not only a life-changing event for the participants, but also for all the 300 fellow pupils who watched it from the auditorium. One student, who worked at a fast-food chain during the day, went on to play the title role in *Orpheus* and continues his links with the opera house today. As his confidence grows, there is no doubt that hamburgers and chips will one day give way to a future of caviar and asparagus tips for this bold young man!

A Tudor day

Less ambitious school-based projects inspired by a topic can also lend themselves to a multidimensional arts approach. I was involved in a 'Tudor Day' with an entire year 6 group, where each child and teacher was assigned a role, such as cook, alchemist, etc., and wore the appropriate Tudor costume. Even visitors had to don a cloak and assume an active role. As the classrooms were transformed into Tudor houses, the morning session involved the children working on the crafts of the day and the afternoon focused on leisure pursuits, including Tudor songs and dances. The children assumed the language of Tudor England, addressing each other as 'Mistress' and 'Master', and successfully stayed in character throughout the day. All inhibition was abandoned as normally self-conscious boys and girls were dancing hand-in-hand, delighting in each other's company. The children were enthralled and transported by the experience. It was a day that will, undoubtedly, stand out in the children's memories as one of their best school experiences.

Shakespeare

I have also undertaken Shakespeare with a junior school drama group, using excerpts from *Macbeth* and *A Midsummer Night's Dream*. The idea of introducing Shakespeare to ten-year-olds might seem overambitious and inappropriate, but it entirely depends on finding an approach to fit the children's age. Using Leon Garfield's *Animated Tales* series to introduce *Macbeth*, I adapted Garfield's script to create a mini-version

109

of the 'Scottish Play'. Music and dance played a prominent place in the production, which featured the 'Danse de Phryne' from *Faust* by Gounod and 'The Witches' Dance' from Purcell's *Dido and Aeneas*. For the mechanicals' play ('The Tragedy of Pyramus and Thisbe') from *A Midsummer Night's Dream*, I edited the scene and used music from *La Bayadère* by Minkus and a Bergomask dance.

Just what these young thespians gained from their introduction to Shakespeare is best expressed by a ten-year-old member in the group:

> 'When I first started Shakespeare I didn't like it at all. It was frightening and scary. One night I went home and cried because I thought I couldn't do it. That night I even had vivid dreams about it. But after a while I began to change my mind. Step by step, the stories made sense and I found myself feeling older and older as I understood it better. Gradually, it began to feel that a part of me that I'd never known before was taking over. I'm no longer scared of Shakespeare and it's a lot more fun than maths!'

Children as dreamers

While it is satisfying for devotees of the arts to see children fulfilling their dreams in this way, there are teachers who actively discourage their pupils from dreaming. A dreamer can often get the tag of someone who has poor concentration and is lacking in academic focus. But if human beings are not afforded the opportunity to dream when they are young, what chance do they have of fulfilling their dreams as adults? It's often the dreamy children who are most capable of accessing their true feelings, emotions and imagination. While they may not always win their teachers' approval, they might well become the visionaries of tomorrow!

Children have a natural and instinctive desire to want to fulfil their whole capacity for living, not just their intellectual potential. They see adults gradually alienating themselves from nature in an effort to control and dominate it. They look to their parents and teachers to help them 'feel' the learning experience in a bid to rekindle the underlying patterns of nature. They recognise that science needs to lose its exploitative means-to-an-end element in favour of meeting the full range of real human needs.

Very often, a school's vision statement will include a few philosophical words about the importance of pupils' social–emotional development and make mention of nurturing a greater awareness of self but, in reality, there's rarely any tangible evidence of this going on. There is still too much focus on the cognitive and very little on the feelings connected with it. Most lessons on feelings are merged into other lessons in the hope that they will somehow be dealt with, but we cannot leave emotional lessons to chance.

A humanistic approach to teaching

While emotional literacy needs to be part of a whole school policy and integral to every subject within the curriculum, children also need timetabled classes which focus on emotional issues to help them recognise and name their emotions. They need to establish an emotional vocabulary so that they can interpret and understand the causes and effects of their actions on themselves and others. This should include lessons in how to listen and collaborate, how to manage their feelings and deal with stress, how to be responsible for their own actions and how to resolve a conflict and negotiate a compromise, as well as showing respect and empathy towards others. It would also embrace anger-management strategies, such as learning to be assertive rather than aggressive and confrontational.

In addition to specifically targeted times, teachers need to adopt a humanistic approach to every lesson, so that pupils feel safe to share their feelings and emotions rather than being isolated and alienated from them. This includes a commitment on the part of teachers to share their own feelings. Teachers cannot expect pupils to give without receiving. This includes fostering an unconditionally high regard for all pupils, thus allowing them to be themselves. In an environment that is free of external evaluation and judgements, pupils will grow to feel valued no matter what they say or do.

So many children are afraid to express their emotions for fear of being ridiculed or laughed at by their peers. But if teachers can instil in their pupils that caring and sharing, empathy and sensitivity, are just as important as reading and writing, then their fears will gradually be transformed into trust. A teacher with a positive and upbeat outlook, someone who can create a warm and supportive ambiance in the classroom, can easily help pupils to become more comfortable about expressing and handling their feelings. If all children grow in the knowledge that their thoughts and feelings are important then school will become important to them. The classroom will then represent a safe haven for all children as they experience a greater sense of belonging. They will then be more likely to behave in a manner that is socially acceptable.

What we so often fail to acknowledge as teachers is that pupils' feelings are always present in the learning process. How children feel about what they are learning has a direct influence on how they learn. It follows that the better children feel about themselves and others, the more they are likely to achieve. It is vitally important that we help all children to think and act through their feelings, which involves not merely skimming the surface of their emotions but getting in touch with what is authentic and individual in each and every one of them.

Let there be light

If we are to develop as a species and realise our full potential, we can no longer afford to ignore the feelings and stifle the emotions of our children. Parents and teachers have an obligation to nurture children's senses and sensibilities. For our education system to move out of the darkness and into the light, it's imperative that it incorporates the arts in harmony with the sciences to help children develop an appreciation of the beauty and abundance of the world they study that will ultimately lead them to a higher moral and spiritual awareness. It will also enable them to develop an understanding of others within their own culture and beyond. For the sake of future generations, now is the time to let the children sing.

Some may see my vision as only possible in a utopian world, but if children are given an opportunity for their souls to be properly nurtured so that they can authentically express their own voices and sing their own songs, as adults they will have a greater sense of peace and contentment, which they will also be able to share with others. Out of their new-found serenity and ability to meditate, which will become a blissful rather than a fearful state of being, they will be able to live a richer and more fulfilled existence, a seemingly unattainable goal that we can only get glimpses of in the present chaos of our emotionally crippled reality.

PART TWO

Feeling the Way Ahead

During the course of writing this book, I undertook many interviews and was presented with opinions from children's services, children, parents, teachers, classroom assistants, head teachers, university professors, educationists, educational psychologists and psychotherapists on how we might better enable young people to gain more fulfilment and enjoyment from their home lives and school environments in relation to greater awareness of emotional development and the nurturing of feelings. Here are just a few of the valuable contributions.

Alison Murphy was, until recently, director of children's services at ChildLine, the UK's free helpline for children in trouble or danger, open 24 hours a day, every day. Trained volunteer counsellors offer comfort, advice and protection to children who may feel they have nowhere else to turn. Since it was launched in 1986, ChildLine has saved children's lives, broken paedophile rings, found refuges for children in danger on the streets and given hope to thousands of children who believed no one else cared for them.

'Last year (1 April 2002 to 31 March 2003) over 14,500 children spoke to ChildLine about family relationship problems, which are the second most common single reason for young people getting in touch with ChildLine. Children who call ChildLine about family relationships describe a whole range of problems from relatively minor arguments with parents or siblings, to serious breakdowns within their families. Often these problems reflect transitions and changes that families go through, such as a new baby in the family or an older sibling leaving home. Some children are deeply upset by parental separation or divorce, or are finding it difficult to adjust to new relationships with stepfamily members. They often feel they cannot talk to their parents or do not want to cause them more worry.

'Peter (12) told his ChildLine counsellor that his dad had found out that his mum has been having an affair. "They started arguing and he kicked her in the stomach. I just ran out of the house. I don't want to go back."

'Fifteen-year-old Kira told ChildLine her parents were really angry when they found out that she had a boyfriend. "They shouted at me and called me a slut. Now they won't let me out of the house except to go to school."

'Ellie (14) said, "Dad isn't speaking to me and I hate it. I came home drunk after a party at Christmas and since then he's been hard on me. He no longer trusts me and

117

won't listen to me. I just want him to love me like he used to."

'Steven (12) said, "Mum's started shouting at me, she calls me stupid and makes me cry ... she's got a new job and it makes her tired."

'Last year, over 8,500 children were counselled by ChildLine about sexual abuse, which represents 7% of the total number of children counselled. Of these children, 6,356 were girls and 2,184 were boys. Fifty-nine per cent of children who spoke to a ChildLine counsellor about sexual abuse said the perpetrator of the abuse was a member of their family (24% said they had been abused by their father – this is by far the largest "category" of perpetrator that children spoke about to ChildLine). Thirty-two per cent said the perpetrator was someone they knew outside the family. Five per cent of children counselled about sexual abuse said the perpetrator was a stranger, while a further 5% did not, or were unable to, tell the counsellor who had abused them. Sadly, children can often feel that they are to blame and it can take several calls before a child explains what is really happening.

'Ten-year-old Julie said, "My dad sometimes takes me out after school. Mum doesn't know, but he always comes with another man and they touch me. It hurts, but I can't stop them. Dad said he will kill mum if I tell anyone."

'Emma (16) said, "My mum and dad make me have sex with men for money. My dad takes my clothes off and then the men jump on me. I tried to get away once but my dad dragged me back by my hair." Emma had informed the police about what was happening to her but she said they did not believe her. She said that she had bruises on her arms, legs and face because of being forced to have sex.

'Kelly (15) rang to say that her mum's boyfriend kept coming on to her. She told her mum, who accused her of leading him on. Kelly was really frightened about what would happen when he came home later that night. With

Kelly's permission, the counsellor contacted social services on her behalf, and they arranged for her to stay with relatives. ChildLine subsequently heard that social services and the child protection team were undertaking an investigation into Kelly's situation.

'Last year, for the seventh year running, bullying was the most common single reason for children and young people to speak to ChildLine's counsellors – 18% of the children helped UK-wide. ChildLine spoke to over 21,800 children about bullying – 16,533 girls and 5,333 boys (the ratio of girls to boys calling ChildLine overall is just over 3:1).

'Of the types of bullying reported by children, 63% was for name calling, 48% was for physical bullying, 9% for verbal or written threats, 7% for extortion, 2% for isolation, 4% for racism and 2% for sexual bullying.

'Greg (11) was terrified of going back to school on Monday. "This group of boys come and find me every play time. They hit me, punch me, drag me around the playground and tear up my work. I'm always getting into trouble with the teachers for looking scruffy and not handing in my homework." Greg told the counsellor that he had horrible nightmares every Sunday. "I feel as if I can't ever get away from them – they wait for me after school. Last Friday I was hiding in the changing rooms and they found me and blocked the door. One of them had a knife." The boys had threatened to "batter him on Monday".

'Fifteen-year-old Shamila called in tears saying that she dreaded going to school. She told the counsellor how she used to be outgoing but she "didn't like talking much now". For the past month, Shamila had been bullied by a gang of girls in her class because, she said, "I'm about the only Asian girl in my school." Shamila explained that she couldn't talk to her parents about how she was feeling because her mum and dad were not getting on very well and she did not want to add to their worries.

'Billy (8). "I can't go to school, I just can't," said Billy through his sobs. He had just jumped off the school bus to call ChildLine. Other children on the bus had been teasing him, snatching his school bag, throwing things at him, thumping him on the head and in the chest and calling him names.

'Fourteen-year-old Jackie was desperately upset when she called ChildLine. A girl who used to be her best friend had turned against her and was now calling her names and making her life "hell". Jackie said, "I took an overdose a couple of months ago. I just wanted someone to notice me – to notice the bullying."

'All of the details in this interview are taken from real calls to ChildLine. They are representative of the kinds of things that children and young people tell ChildLine. All names and identifying details have been changed to protect the callers.'

Eileen Hayes is parenting adviser for The National Society for the Prevention of Cruelty to Children (NSPCC). It is the UK's leading charity specialising in child protection and the prevention of cruelty to children.

'We know from research and our own work with parents that many find it hard to think beyond the birth of their baby. We advise all parents-to-be to give themselves an emotional health check. While they are getting their house or flat ready for the baby, we suggest that they take a few minutes to think about getting their 'emotional house' ready, too. We point out that as well as the exciting, looking-forward feelings that parents-to-be experience, pregnancy and parenting can also be a time of scary 'Can I cope? Will my world change forever?' feelings. Most people have heard of the 'baby blues' or postnatal depression but aren't prepared for feeling down during pregnancy and/or for the first few months after giving birth. In some ways, they may never have felt happier, but roughly one in ten mothers will feel low at least some of the time. It's common to ask, 'Will I be a good enough mother?' or worry, 'Will my baby be OK?' It's also common for dads to wonder why they don't always feel on top of the world at the prospect of becoming a father. Getting these issues out in the open can help parents consider where they might experience difficulties and who they might go to for help.

'Pregnancy can stir up fears and feelings that have been hidden for years. A mother-to-be can find herself thinking, 'What on earth have I done?' or 'What am I letting myself in for?' If she felt her own mum and dad didn't do such a great job bringing her up, she might feel worried about making the same mistakes. Having a baby can bring back strong memories of childhood. While some may be good, others may not be so good. We advise mothers-to-be not to bottle up sad or angry memories, to think about whether there were problems in their past that haven't been resolved and to consider whether they now agree with everything about their own upbringing. We point out that parenting styles may have changed and that, while their parents probably did the best they could at the time, there may have been areas that need to be discussed and worked on.

'Mothers need a great deal of love and support, ideally from the person who's helped to make the baby. If this is not possible, then it is important to have support from other adult members of the family or friends. Any misunderstandings and sources of conflict need to be sorted out before the baby comes along because it is important not to have their arguments over the baby's head.

'Expectant parents need to work on managing their anger before they are faced with the stresses a baby inevitably brings, which means being honest. In the first instance, they need to accept that anger is a normal human emotion. They can then work out whether there might be underlying anger which has stemmed from being pushed into becoming a parent or whether they are experiencing resentment about being used or not wanted.

'It is important for mothers-to-be to find ways to cut down stress by listening to music, getting plenty of exercise, being pampered and practising the pregnancy relaxation and breathing exercises to keep them calm and serene. All prospective mums get anxious from time to time, but recent research has shown that extreme anxiety can cut down on the amount of blood going to the uterus which can result in a premature or smaller-than-normal baby.

'Whatever family structure children are born into, they need to feel welcome and secure. It needs to be recognised that growing up with only one parent can be a positive experience, and children may have an especially close relationship with that parent. Children of lone parents need to be given a sense of pride in being part of a single-parent family so that they don't feel second best. Even so, it's important to let children spend time with their other parent, too. Most children want to understand about how both their parents fit in with their lives. All children have a right to know who their parents are and to know that it's OK to love both parents without feeling guilty. It's important that children do not become substitutes for adult companions. Parents need to find other adults to share any worries and not to use children as emotional crutches.

'If a baby is being born into an existing stepfamily, there may be some interesting extra challenges. Children from the old family may have very mixed feelings. It may be the first time they really owned up to the fact that their own parents are not getting back together. Existing children need to feel that they are just as important as a new baby. It is also important to bear in mind that teenage children are unpredictable and might not be too keen on having a new baby in the family. In addition, there can sometimes be tension from grandparents and other relatives, who can have mixed feelings about the baby of the new partnership. It is important to understand a partner's strong connections with previous children, and time needs to be allowed to maintain such relationships.'

'Once the baby arrives, it is important how parents respond to their baby's cry. They need to realise that crying is a baby's main language and it's designed to help them survive. Responding to a new baby's cry quickly helps them feel the world is a safe friendly place. Research indicates that babies cry less later on if their cries are answered straightaway in the early stages of their development. Knowing there will always be someone to care for them helps babies develop self-esteem and grow into confident children.

'But crying can make parents feel very anxious. Some parents find crying very hard to bear, especially if it is persistent. They may even hit or shake their babies. If crying ever makes a parent feel that they really can't cope and that there is a danger of taking it out on the baby, it is vital to get help. We advise a parent in this position to put the baby down gently somewhere safe like a cot or pram; go into another room and sit down for a few minutes; take a deep breath and let it out slowly; turn on the TV or radio if it helps to distract their mind; ask a friend or relative to take over for a while and, once they feel calmer, to go back to the baby. We produce a leaflet called "Handle with Care" and a fact sheet which gives advice on coping with persistent crying.

'Of course, a baby requires practical things but there are emotional things that they need more, especially unconditional love. If you can love your child without expecting anything in return, they grow up feeling more confident and positive about themselves and are more able to love others.'

Daniel Richardson is a lively and outspoken ten-year-old who attends a small Church of England school in East Sussex.

'The best thing about school is friends and play times. The trouble at our school is that we don't get long enough play times. As soon as the bell goes for break, it seems like we're lining up and going back to class for more work. Teachers don't seem to understand that kids love play and mixing with their friends. This is the best part of the day. Also, we need PE every day. Our classroom's very hot. We need more time to breathe better. Children sometimes get loony when they don't get enough fresh air. They also get very bored sitting at a desk for too many hours. There's too much literacy, numeracy and science and not enough of the good stuff. It all goes on for far too long and we never get a break. Every day's the same – work, work, work!

'We need more things like history, making things and discovering things for ourselves. We also need more visits to interesting places. I still remember a visit to Hever Castle in Year 4. It was really cool. I could imagine the kings and queens of the past walking through the posh rooms and sleeping in their four-poster beds. This year we went on a residential trip for a week. That was also great – visiting all the places connected with the Battle of Hastings during the day and playing games like pool and table tennis in the evening with all my mates. We got to go to bed really late and visit each other's rooms. It would be good to go on more visits and have less time at school. We learn better when we're away from school because there aren't so many rules and it's a lot freer. Our teachers are also nicer outside school. We can play tricks on them and they don't get upset!

'At school, teachers don't have a lot of time to listen to kids. They often whine on about nothing. They can also be grumpy and moody. If you tell them about a problem you might be having, they'll often say, "Don't tell tales!' They don't seem to have time to listen to our problems 'cos they're always getting ready for the next lesson. They also blame you for things you haven't done. You can sometimes do a couple of bad things and then you get a reputation and get picked on. You don't always feel like going in in the morning because you know you're going to get punished for something you haven't done. Sometimes this makes you feel like you're not very important, a bit like a robot, something that gets switched on and off when the teacher says so.

'I can't understand why there aren't more men in school. We see them outside but we never see them here. Women are always chatting and fussing. Men prefer a bit of action. We need them to do more games with us. The vicar in the church is a man and he goes on for hours praying and saying the same old words. Even though it's a bit cold, I like the atmosphere in church, but the kids don't always understand what's going on.

'I also think it would be fairer if we weren't put into groups for subjects, because it makes some children feel useless at their work. Everybody's good at something, but if they're not very good at the things we're tested on, like writing, maths and science, they lose heart and give up on the things they can do. This Easter we all made cards for our families. Everybody's was good but only two kids, one boy and one girl, got special Easter egg prizes for theirs, because the teacher said theirs were the best. I think with something like that, everyone needs to be treated the same because everybody tried the same to make theirs good. Easter's about when Jesus died on the cross. He was the kind of man who would have shared things out equally and not made some children feel more special than the others.

'Schools need to understand our feelings more. Everyone

has feelings. Boys and girls have the same feelings deep down. When boys get told off, they hide their feelings because they've got to be tough and girls let it all out. If you call girls nasty names they tend to get upset and cry, but boys who get called names either ignore it or come up with even nastier language. Then they get accused of being aggressive when they aren't really. A child's feelings are more important than the education they get. If you say nasty things to someone they hurt inside but if you say nasty things about education it can't hurt the system because it's not a living thing. Education can't hurt inside like I can.'

Alex Williams is a 16-year-old student at a school with performing arts status. I have known her since year 5, when we worked together on a drama project. She is currently preparing for her GCSEs.

'Schools put too much pressure on children to achieve and get exam results. It's all too competitive and we'll never do our best if we're being judged according to someone else's yardstick. It's a lot easier for those who are exam-oriented and will come out on top, but even they feel under constant pressure and sometimes crack. I'm forever feeling that I have to live up to other people's expectations. I think it's enough to have tried your best for yourself. The pressure to achieve for others is an unnecessary evil.

'Even in my primary school I felt pressure to conform, to fit in to what my teachers and peers expected of me. I hated my primary school because I didn't fit in to the nice, neat square box that they wanted to put me in. I was never afraid to express my opinion and I got a reputation for being bolshy, someone not very nice to deal with. From my perspective, I was saying what I thought. I look back now and realise that what I had to say was valid even though my opinions were nearly always discounted. I believe there's always a simple solution, but I was being led down a complicated path, which confused me.

'I was always getting into trouble for petty things like having a bag of sweets in my lunch box on my birthday. It was confiscated and never returned to me. Also, I had a pencil case that was a bit bigger than normal and I couldn't quite close my drawer. The teacher didn't like it because it stuck out more than anyone else's. I was told to get a smaller pencil case. There was too much emphasis on the superficial and not nearly enough on what really mattered, which was our education. Fortunately, there was a music teacher who understood me. She always found time to explain things and valued what I had to say.

'The worst part of my early schooling was being bullied by two girls from reception to year 5. For six years I was on the receiving end of constant verbal taunting. I was called "fat", "ugly", "thick", and told I wasn't going to get anywhere in life. I'd cry myself to sleep. It was nasty and unnecessary. I always loved going to school because I enjoyed learning, but the breaks and lunchtimes were intolerable. I told my parents what I was going through and they tried to teach me how to be a stronger person and defend myself. It was only after I was punched in the face that they came to the school, but nothing was done. The teachers told me to "stop telling tales"!

'At the time I thought I was the problem. As I look back now, I realise that it was the bullies who had the problem. They had low self-esteem and used me as a scapegoat for their insecurities. They needed to put me down to elevate themselves. But at the time I felt I had no choice but to try another junior school, which was the best thing I could have done. At my new school, the teachers treated me much more like an individual than a statistic. It was altogether a happier place, more human, less middle class and less daunting in terms of what was expected of me.

'I was devastated when one of the bullies from my first primary school followed me to secondary school and started taunting me all over again. I decided to have some counselling about it and it made me realise I wasn't the one with the problem. I was taught strategies to avoid being a victim or becoming a bully myself. We all have the potential to upset others. Sometimes I'm cold and unreceptive to people, which must make them feel uncomfortable. I've found in my life that shutting down can be an easier way to deal with problems than facing them head-on. As I mature, I hope to find ways to deal with things more assertively. At the moment my sensitivity always seems to get the better of me.

'I think being sensitive and being in touch with my feelings actually worked against me when I was younger. My father isn't very good at showing his emotions, but my mother is more like me and is able to express her emotions more freely. I first realised how sensitive I was at the age of eight, when my mother and grandmother had a big falling out. My grandmother was fun and outgoing but she carried a dark secret. She was sexually abused by her father, which made her incapable of relating to her own children. She saw it as acceptable for her husband, my grandfather, to do the same to my mother. Since my mother confronted my grandmother on it, the two have never spoken. My mother obviously felt a terrible sense of betrayal and was angry with my grandmother for not protecting her from my grandfather. Their feud has always given me a deep-rooted inability to trust people. I always feel that they will inevitably let me down or abandon me.

'The rift between my mother and grandmother upset me a great deal when I was very young because then I didn't know or understand the cause. Today, I feel sad that I can't have a relationship with my grandmother. When my grandfather died last year, it brought all the pain back again. It felt wrong to grieve because it wasn't my grief. It felt wrong to hate because it wasn't my hate. It felt wrong to love because I'd never known my grandfather. I only know what he did!

'I suppose this experience has given me a lot more empathy and compassion for people. We all carry a lot of pain. I look at some of my friends' lives and I know how much they suffer, some from their parents' divorces, some from seeing their dads beating up their mums, some from never knowing their dads. And yet none of this is taken into consideration at school. Sometimes children aren't able to do their work or behave well because they're too emotionally distressed or bereft. There may be something

130

preying on their mind, such as a death in the family or a quarrel with a parent or a friend. Teachers don't always take their pupils' feelings seriously enough. They look at things on face value and don't have the time to probe a little deeper. They have no idea what pressure young people experience trying to juggle their personal and school lives.

'Fortunately, my life is now going well. My secondary school, which specialises in the performing arts, has put me on the right track. I honestly believe that my present teachers are dedicated to helping me realise who I am and what I want to be. It all began in year 7 when I took up singing, which changed my outlook on life. It's given me a reason to be. Nothing is better than singing knowing everyone in the room is listening, appreciating and validating me. I know it's something that I do well and I'm happy to be judged by it. I also love acting and dancing. Acting has given me a lot of confidence and it's helped me to be more comfortable with myself. The more comfortable you are with yourself the more effectively you can portray someone else. I've also learned a lot about myself through dance, which I've found a very liberating experience.

'The arts are very important in school because they not only give you the opportunity to express yourself, they also give you the confidence to speak your mind in other areas of the curriculum. Unfortunately, they're very low on the priority list in most schools because a career in the arts is not seen as realistic or sensible. But as far as I'm concerned they are a vital way of getting to know yourself better which, after all, is the most important thing in life!'

Paul Fielding is a 16-year-old student who is studying for his GCSEs and a year 11 representative on his school council.

'My parents were pretty devastated when I was born with a cleft palate. I don't know whether it was anything to do with this birth defect, which was repaired a year after I was born, but from an early age I can never recall my parents hugging me or feeling that they loved me unconditionally. I'm the youngest of three children and always felt a bit different from my older brother and sister. Unlike other boys, I hated toy guns and action men. I always felt that my father severely disliked me because I had more of an interest in dolls and dressing up. My father and I have a very similar temperament. We're both very stubborn and argumentative. I don't think he was ever that struck with babies. Apparently, when we were all young he used to say, "I'll like them when they grow up!"

'I think my father would like me to have been a bit more like him. He's very keen on sports, especially rugby. At school, he was always getting into fights and got a lot of detentions. He was definitely one of the lads. Although I'm good at swimming and athletics, I've never liked contact sports. I'd really like it if my dad could accept me for exactly who I am and not what he'd like me to be. In general, I find male relationships quite difficult. I can remember having a long-term friendship with a boy at infant school and I now have male associates but, generally, I don't get on with boys. I much prefer female company and all my best friends are girls.

'I've also always liked and respected older people. In fact, my best friend is my spiritual healer, a woman of 55 whom I met at the spiritual church that I belong to. Although I was christened in the Church of England faith, I'm one of those people who believe that all the major religions have something to offer. I am able to embrace elements of the teachings of Allah, Buddha and Jesus in harmony with all sorts of alternative practices and beliefs including re-incarnation, clairvoyance, dreams and crystals. For me, they're all part of the same big picture. I'm sure many people would think I was slightly mad, but I believe that anything that helps you discover more about yourself, the world you inhabit and what might lie beyond, the better.

'I'd like to see the curriculum opening up a bit to embrace not just the conventional but also the unconventional religions and rituals in our society. It encourages greater tolerance and empathy in young people. The problem is a lot of teachers aren't that open to new ideas. Quite a few are not completely secure within themselves and are on a power trip. It's a pity that they couldn't be a bit more relaxed and less obsessed with being in control, which they often think is best achieved by yelling at us. One of the things kids hate most is shouting. I'm not sure why teachers need to raise their voices quite so much when most things can be achieved or resolved much more quickly and effectively in a calm and rational way.

'While many teachers are happy to simply impart their subject, fortunately there are a few who understand children have emotional needs, too. I have a particular language teacher who will see someone looking a bit down and ask them "Are you OK? Is there anything I can do?" What's a bit sad is that teachers often fail to realise that what a pupil is outwardly projecting may not be exactly what they're feeling inside. They put on a front to hide what they're really feeling. The laws of projection and reflection are quite interesting. What you project onto people is what they reflect back onto you. In that sense, we all mirror each other. We all have aspects of our personalities that we recognise in others. Sometimes this can trigger a positive response, sometimes a negative response.

'I'm one of those people who challenges and questions everything. It's never a matter of seeing things in terms of black or white but in shades of grey, and considering all angles. A lot of what we're being asked to accept in the classroom is based on absolutes and dogma. Young people need more opportunities to express their own opinions and work things out for themselves. I'm unable to go along with something because it's being asked of me, I have to understand and believe in what I'm getting involved in.

'Most kids will conform simply to fit in with the majority. They'll do anything for a bit of street cred from their peers. I've never been able to follow the group, the group has always followed me. Although I'm not a sheep, I feel there's a place for me within the flock. Our society not only needs more people who have strong views, but it also needs to be more accepting of individuals who are not afraid to speak the truth and express an opinion.

'Most of my peers think teachers are the enemy and are unable to see them as real human beings. But if they looked a bit closer, they would see a caring and fascinating group of people who are wanting to impart and share their knowledge and experiences. I'm sure teachers would be able to give a lot more if they weren't so overburdened with red tape and a need to meet targets. As far as I'm concerned, the only targets they need to meet are those which provide them with a sense of satisfaction for helping to shape the thoughts and feelings of the next generation!'

Julie Bennett has been teaching for twenty years, nine in the secondary sector and eleven in the junior. For the first time in her career, she recently decided to take a break from teaching. She has two teenage daughters.

'I went into teaching because I like children and enjoy relating to them as individuals. I've always felt that it's a people job and if you don't like people you shouldn't do it. But in the last few years, I've been feeling more and more that it's become a job where people's feelings are beginning to matter less. Education seems to be moving away from the idea of focusing on the interests of children as unique human beings with specific needs and becoming much more to do with turning them into products that have to be targeted, judged and assessed. The pendulum has swung in such a way that there's too much pressure on children and teachers to raise academic standards and meet targets.

'I had always enjoyed teaching English, which is my specialist subject, until the introduction of the Literacy Hour. It was structured in such a rigid and restrictive way that I found it didn't suit my teaching style. Not only did I find the Literacy Hour to be characterised by too much heavy direction – which is thankfully now beginning to ease off a little – but it wasn't fulfilling the children's needs. For instance, for children to be able to write a good story they need resources of creative inspiration, but the Literacy Hour didn't seem to be encouraging these. By teaching to a formula, both the children and the teachers were missing out on originality and spontaneity. I always felt that the Numeracy Hour was more realistic in its aims and objectives. It offers a lot more flexibility and provides the children and teachers with a bit more creative scope. I find it more punchy and flexible, allowing room for manoeuvrability.

'One of the best things about teaching is being able to offer children seeds of ideas upon which they can build their own creations. I like the idea of equality and cooperation in the creative process. When something works, it is usually because both the teacher and the children have been equally inspired and energised by a project. When teaching is too directed by the teacher, the children lose interest. Children must feel that they've made a valid contribution to their learning, otherwise they don't feel as though they own it.

'But a teacher also needs to feel fulfilled as a creative artist. In the last few years, I found myself getting bound up with all the precise paperwork for external evaluation, when a few scribbled notes would have served me just as well. I found the two hours daily set aside for literacy and numeracy left very little time for anything else. I was tired of having to substantiate and justify everything. I found my creative energy was being dissipated and I was being forced into areas which took me away from opportunities to bond with the children. In a sense, I felt I was losing my personality along with my sense of humour and an ability to laugh!

'Once I'd given in my notice, all that changed. In my last half-term of teaching, I felt I was able to laugh again and resume teaching for teaching's sake, because the constant pressure was at last off. When teachers are relaxed and happy they are of much more value to children. Children are so incredibly needy that, when they sense their teacher is under pressure, they can suffer quite badly. Children definitely learn more readily when they're comfortable and relaxed. This is why I think it's so important for teachers to work from where children actually are and not from where others who are planning the curriculum think they might be. I think it's also vitally important that children have less physical restriction, fewer lessons at desks and more opportunities for movement. There also has to be room for spontaneity.

'Unless there are equal opportunities for planned and unplanned responses within the curriculum, children are in

136

danger of getting a lopsided education. I have a particular interest in teaching dance. I don't remember all that much about my first attempts, except that I must have been feeling brave and had a go. I had had no formal dance training but decided to take a chance and see where it would lead. It is now one of my favourite subjects and the children often get so much from it because it allows them an outlet for their feelings and emotions. Dance releases tensions, it's a shared and cooperative experience and has a definite feel-good factor.

'While it's an essentially physical experience involving the body, it also engages the mind. It can be particularly helpful for children who have difficulty with academic work. In fact, I frequently find that children who cannot express things very easily in words have the most affinity with dance.

'I tend to teach dance in half-term blocks and might start with a piece of music that I've enjoyed, e.g. the theme music from the film *American Beauty*. I'll ask the children to think about what they've heard, to move to it, and then encourage them to interpret their thoughts while they're moving. We then take some of these ideas and develop them on an individual basis, with a partner or within a group. I am always amazed at what children are capable of and yet we so often deny them the opportunity to express their creativity in this kind of way.

'One of the last dance projects I worked on was with a year 5 class. We'd been studying myths in the Literacy Hour and decided to invent our own myth and adapt it to a dance/drama. Some of it was choreographed and some of it improvised. We decided to show it in assembly and invite the parents in. The children used their IT skills to make posters to advertise the event and it became a cross-curricular project.

'Children invariably enjoy and learn a great deal from

these kind of multidimensional experiences. It's not only the final performance that matters to them but the evolution of the creative process, observing how others are involved and analysing what personal contribution they're making. I think children need more opportunities for projects which bring the arts together in a meaningful and purposeful way.'

Michael Edwards is a former care officer at The Cotswold Therapeutic Community for emotionally disturbed teenage boys and now a teacher specialising in design technology. He has two young children who are home-schooled. He believes the present education system causes undue stress and depression for parents, teachers and pupils alike. His solution is what he calls "human continuum education".

'The idea of human continuum education is only part of a larger "continuum concept" based on the idea that humans, like other animals, have beliefs and expectations concerning all aspects of life. The continuum concept was conceived by Jean Liedloff when she was on holiday in the South American jungle. She came across a tribe who, she felt, acted in ways which the west could learn from. She noted that babies hardly ever cried, there were no "terrible twos" and no antagonistic teenagers. In her book *The Continuum Concept* she claims that as we are a primate species, we need to offer babies as natural a birth as possible, carry our children as much as possible (they expect and therefore need it) and breastfeed on demand. She describes humans as being extremely social animals and that our children act out what we "expect" of them, e.g. if you say to a child, "You'll fall if you climb that tree," they may well act it out to prove their parents right.

'Although Liedloff concentrated on parenting, I believe that what she had to say, the fact that we had a social programme which has been disturbed and lost, could apply to all aspects of the way we live. This altered state of being leaves us confused, even anguished, and leads us to act unreasonably when dealing with everyday situations such as parenting, relationships and education.

'I love working with children, but I feel the present education system breeds discontentment, lack of fulfilment, antisocial behaviour and mediocrity. Forcing all children to do twelve specified subjects, in case they need to call upon them in years to come, is a nonsense. The reality is that we have overweight children bullied into doing 1,500-metre runs to gain experience, dyslexic children forced to learn two foreign languages when they struggle with their own, and the vast majority of young people put off education because they only have an interest in a few of the designated areas of study.

'Children need to be taught according to their interests at a given time. My six-year-old daughter Thea, who is home-schooled, has been allowed to follow her own "unblocked" interests, which I believe is a more natural way of learning. She has already had the practical experiences of tiling a wall, hammering in nails and cutting vegetables, tasks which are usually deemed more appropriate for much older children.

'I'm convinced that school children need freedom to study only the subjects that they are naturally drawn to and not to be forced to suffer those in which they have no interest or natural acumen. If children were allowed to study more of what they were drawn to and less of what they were not, they would feel less victimised, more valued and have a greater opportunity to achieve excellence.

'When curriculum designers first got together, they probably worked on the assumption that it was important to give young people a broad-based education. They assumed that all humans have the ability and capacity to learn a wide range of subjects and recall that knowledge when they come to choose a career. But the truth is that most of us remember very little indeed of what was taught at school. All we retain is what we enjoyed.

'A better approach when looking at curriculum content would be to look at how we can best serve the learner and society in a mutually beneficial way. We retain knowledge best when we live it. While we have the ability to learn quickly and adapt to new situations, the more engrossed we

140

are in a meaningful task the more individuals and others benefit from it.

'For those educationists who favour a broad approach to education, it is perfectly possible to place greater focus on one or two areas and still give breadth. If a school offers a wide range of interesting courses and fun days to try out other curriculum areas, then the breadth is endless. We already see a marked improvement in children's behaviour when they are offered "Activity Weeks", an opportunity for pupils to come off timetable and select from a range of activities. Such experiences engage and empower children to such an extent that they simply forget to misbehave!

'The invention of conventional schooling, which forced children to do many subjects against their will and expected them to be proficient in all areas, even if they were unrelated to the real world, was probably a massive setback for mankind's natural progression and excellence. This enforcement system not only tries to mould individuals into certain expectations which are unnatural and inhuman, it has also proved to be a waste of time and money because so much of the information given to pupils at school is completely lost or forgotten within five or ten years of them leaving. It would all be a lot more cost-effective if each school could be empowered to judge the specific needs of individual pupils and run the curriculum as they saw fit to include vocational courses as well as academic ones.

'Passion for a subject is the most powerful motivator and, when it is present in education, it gets the best results. It is usually associated with excellence and often involves children noticing how challenging things were retrospectively. But passion can be destroyed if impetus is affected. Staggered timetabling and long gaps between subjects can exaggerate and increase the "challenging" bits, as well as diminish children's interest. By the time young people reach adolescence they are confused about their passion(s) and, as a consequence,

141

they are unsure about which career would best suit them. For thousands of years before our present education system existed, most 12-year-olds were already passionate and proficient in a vocational pursuit. It remained with them throughout their lives as a constant source of pleasure and would also benefit others.

'If adults cared more about children's feelings, and not so much about their own dogmas, they would begin to recognise that self-fulfilment is the major prerequisite for children's learning. This leads to excellence which, in turn, nurtures a progressive, highly skilled and well-balanced society able to thrive in a climate of healthy competition. The greatest fear of parents is that their children won't be educated, but their greatest fear needs to be that their children won't have emotional stability.'

Kevin McCarthy has been teaching for 25 years in a range of schools and college settings. He is currently working in the field of creativity as well as providing courses on emotional literacy, teacher well-being and learning styles. He is the author of Learning By Heart: The Role of Emotional Education in Raising School Achievement and has wide knowledge of experiential education. He is founder and director of Re: membering Education and has three children.

'Since the 1870s, there have been two broad aims of education. The first concerns the transmission of a body of knowledge and cultural values from one generation to another and the second the creation of a productive workforce. I don't think education's got much to do with either of these things. For me, it is more closely linked to Carl Rogers' thinking, education as self-actualisation and the nurturing of a fully integrated, whole person embracing the physical, spiritual, emotional and intellectual. And that's what kids so massively want and need right now. Education, today, needs to be about helping kids to make sense of the world and nurturing self-understanding.

'For this to happen, teachers need to be emotionally literate and have greater self-esteem. If they had a higher opinion of themselves they wouldn't take the kind of absurdity of what is being asked of them. Teachers sit back and no matter how many government initiatives come, no matter how absurd they are in relation to children's development, they get on and implement them in an uncomplaining way. Teachers need to remember their collective strength again, recall a time when there was a degree of autonomy, freedom and flexibility in the classroom and to reconnect with what brought them into education in the first place.

'Unless teachers are self-reflective, self-aware, honest about failure and prepared to acknowledge what presses their buttons, education will never develop in the way it needs to. Unless teachers are well, pupils will never be well. Of course, we need teachers who are intelligent but, more importantly, we need teachers who are sensitive. The human relations issues, which are at the heart of teaching, hardly get addressed on courses for student teachers.

'It's all to do with subject knowledge, competence and awareness of the National Curriculum, a tick-box mentality that has driven out and eroded the development of teachers as relating beings. I like the word "relate" because it sums up what teachers do. It's what we do with stories, we relate stories, but it's also to do with how we get on with others.

'At the moment, the only mode of learning that counts is the cognitive mode, the input and understanding of information and the output of examinations which show literary or numerical skills. Even in a subject like drama, which is what I teach, 40% of the marks aren't for how good you are at drama, they're for how good you are at writing about what you did in drama. I had a pupil who's currently in a West End production who did not get an A* in drama. She got a B because she's dyslexic. There's something fundamentally wrong that even in an art exam some of the marks are given for ability to write within a narrow cognitive band. Of course, it's important to think about what you're doing and reflect on things but we also apprehend things through our feelings. We need to be able to license feelings in the classroom, to be able to discuss things with energy, passion and commitment, to bring a sense of beauty and wonder to science, to bring the whole of ourselves, our feeling heart to everything we do in the curriculum.

'There's an awful lot of talk in schools right now about the importance of balancing auditory, visual and kinaesthetic (active) learning. I sense teenagers are desperate to learn by doing real things in the real world, which helps them to gain a greater understanding of themselves and the world in which they live. Boys, in particular, with their tendency to be less compliant than girls, want to learn by "doing" more than anything else. They're active, kinaesthetic, doing-type learners, and yet we are not allowing them enough opportunities to experiment with that mode of learning.

'By judging children purely on their academic performance, we are valuing the 50% who get A to C grades for their GCSEs, but failing the 50% of pupils who don't. In this sense, the entire education system is built on failure. It's very foundations assume a shortage, competing for limited resources, rather than celebrating abundance. What's the point of a child flogging himself to death to raise his grade from an F to an E in a subject in which he has no interest? It does absolutely nothing for his self-esteem.

'The whole school system is a watering down of the traditional, academic, elite education that 5% of the population had 150 years ago. And we've never shaken ourselves loose from that model of education. We need a completely different model now.

'What baffles me most is that, despite electronic registration systems and all the paraphernalia of the information age, schools have remained essentially unchanged for decades. It's those who are currently working on the periphery, with the disapplied, the disaffected, within the Education Action Zones – where it's quite clear that 10% GCSEs is the top whack pupils are ever going to reach – where things are beginning to change. It's often easier for places where the system is in most decay and disintegration for new ideas and innovations to spring up.

'It's time for everyone involved in education to realise that the arts are absolutely fundamental to children's emotional development. And yet we're constantly battling for their survival. Kids' creativity is massively important, and the arts, from music to fine art, out to design and the social arts of drama and dance, are absolutely central to kids' development and need to be right at the heart of the curriculum. If you take drama as an individual subject, it is such a socially developing art, nurturing the ability to stand inside someone else's shoes, play another part, see things from another person's point of view, play it out and then maybe explore the other side by interpreting it in a different way. The nurturing of that kind of sensitivity towards others is hugely empowering. Drama is not just an artistic self-expression, it can also instil discipline.

'In fact, all the arts require and develop discipline in kids and tend to be self-contained, with a beginning, middle and end. The discipline of the arts comes from the task and not the teacher. A pupil cannot do a piece of improvisational drama unless he sets boundaries and a structure. Dance physically coordinates the body. It's the most corporeal, the most embodied of all the arts and does not rely on words. The visual arts develop the eye and a sense of sensitivity to [the] colour, form, shape and texture of the world, as well as fine motor skills. Music, with its sensitising of the ear, the tuning in, has a knock-on effect in nurturing listening skills in the broadest sense. The give and take of playing the simplest duet with another person, the extraordinary toing and froing that takes place, the echoing of a phrase and the picking up of it again, is amazingly sensitising. The arts are so rich in symbolism and yet we have to defend them all the time.

'If you take a topic like the environment, of course it is important for kids to know about the chemistry and science of it. But what's going to matter in terms of making the world more liveable in is not what they understand about the environment. It's going to be about what they do about the environment, which comes from their attitudes, their feelings and their motivations. We have this peculiar thing in Britain where we have education for the head or education for the body. But if we're to continue as a species and preserve the planet we live on, we need to nurture in our

146

schools the idea of education which also includes knowledge-able, caring, sensitive and active citizenship.

'Kids need opportunities to express their feelings about the world, to have a licence to write the poetry of the stars or to draw the flower, rather than the diagram of the flower, in its living wholeness. We all know that science works by what can be measured and quantified on a scale, but what really matters is the sensual response to it: the affective dimension, the feeling dimension, the bodily dimension. What interests me more and more in education is the interplay between thinking, feeling and action. At the moment, we're massively loaded up in the cognitive realm because it can be counted, measured and weighed. But there are vitally important dimensions of the human spirit that cannot be quantified. These also deserve recognition. You cannot quantify persistence, you cannot give a mark for generosity, you cannot measure compassion. What matters most in kids are the human qualities that are beyond measure.'

Craig Nicholson, a former technical support executive in the computer industry, has had ten years experience teaching in the primary sector. He is the father of three boys.

'I have three young sons and my wife and I have tried to create a loving, fun environment where they can speak their mind and argue amongst themselves. If they have a problem, we try to be there to listen and talk about it. They inevitably squabble and fight a lot but we try to reason with them about how it feels to be on the receiving end of aggressive behaviour. One of the most difficult things in our house, at the moment, is an obsession with the Play Station. We're trying to negotiate a variety of activities, to include something musical, something physical, something cerebral, rather than too many hours on a computer. Every so often I lose my temper with them, but I don't smack them. When negotiation breaks down I tend to send them to their rooms to think about what they've done. I try to keep them positive, but I'm not always as patient as I'd like to be, especially after a day's teaching. I think the hardest thing for a parent is consistency over a long period. After all, adults are human, too, and every so often we snap. I think it's fine for our kids to see us angry but it's important not to dump negative feelings on them.

'Just as my own kids appreciate positive input, it's very important for teachers to stay positive and upbeat. I can remember a colleague saying to me once, "When a teacher walks through the classroom door, he's selling learning. You need to be enthusiastic, bouncing and full of energy." In my view, an important part of being a good teacher is to be a happy person. You can't pretend to be happy, because the kids will soon pick up on it. I think we owe it to the children to have a smile on our faces, but it's not so easy when you've been up half the night marking books. Of course, it's much easier to be happy if the environment of

148

the school is pleasant. Bright, spacious classrooms overlooking green, open fields are much easier to work in than small rundown classrooms surrounded by concrete. Teachers also need a supportive management structure that does its best to make sure that staff are happy.

'A teacher overburdened with paperwork is less likely to be as content as one doing a solid 45-hour week but leaving the job, and more importantly the paperwork, at school. Above all, teachers need to see an end to their day's work. We need to have a situation where after working from eight in the morning until five-thirty in the evening, we can go home in the knowledge that our evenings, weekends and holidays are relatively free. Unless this happens, children will ultimately lose out.

'As far as pupils are concerned, learning has to be fun. There needs to be less emphasis on passing exams, attainment levels and statistics and more focus on kids' emotional well-being, how they treat each other, relate to the world and solve problems. One of the fundamental problems with education is that it all starts too early. There are many children who are simply not ready to start school until they're seven. They need to be running around in a forest and convening with nature. Some nursery schools in Norway take children at four but the day is spent outdoors. They go on to formal education at seven. It's interesting that when test results were recently compared in Britain and Norway, eight-year-old children performed the same!

'Considering children are deskbound for such long periods, I think the vast majority behave incredibly well, especially if we are to believe that a child's attention span is about 15 minutes. In general, adults need to be more accepting and understanding of children's behaviour, especially boys, who have different energy levels and ways of interacting. I think if we learnt to go with the children, listened to their opinions and went at their pace a bit more, rather than trying to knock them into shape quite so much, we might have more success. Of course, there's not nearly enough opportunity for children to offload their physical energy within the constraints of the existing curriculum. A recent research project set up by the University of Exeter gave controlled groups of boys varying amounts of PE. They found that the boys who had the most PE sessions per week significantly outperfomed the others in the classroom. The pupils who took part in sport at least three times a week were more likely to obtain good exam results, and negative behaviour was also reduced. As research tests like these are done and examined, we need to learn from them and be brave enough to adjust the National Curriculum accordingly.

'Teaching's all about being sensitive to individual kids' needs, which is sometimes hard when you're dealing with thirty-four. I often get confused and sometimes hit the wrong nail on the wrong head. In cases like these, the teacher needs to say "sorry" and apologise to the child. For instance, the other day a boy came in and shoved a note in my hand. I put it in my pocket and completely forgot about it. Later that day, I was going through the homework tray. We were having a bit of a blitz on homework and I went down the register to see who hadn't given in their geography.

'The first kid on my list who hadn't handed it in was Jamie and I asked him where it was. He usually did his homework and he was actually the wrong kid to be singling out. When he started crying, I immediately got on to the next name. At the end of the lesson, I took Jamie to one side and said, "I'm sorry, you're a good kid, you always get your homework in on time, it's no big deal." Later on that evening I put my hand in my pocket and pulled out the note, which read, *Sorry Mr Nicholson, Jamie hasn't done his homework because his Grandad's dying.* I felt so bad. The next day I apologised to him again and told him I hadn't read the note. He said it was OK. Of course it wasn't, but I think he really appreciated me saying "sorry". Teachers do make mistakes and they have to model to the kids by example.

'Although I've had quite a bit of experience as a teacher and have three kids of my own, I still feel I'm only scratching the surface of relating to them in a meaningful way. What's really sad is that I don't have enough time to think about what I'm doing and reflect on it. I tend to act on instinct in the hope that I'm getting it halfway right. I go home, mark books, get the plans out, but I don't have time to sit and think about the children, what really makes them tick and whether they're happy.

'I think we could bring a lot more joy to children's learning if there was a greater emphasis on the arts. I think music's really important in helping children emotionally, which is why I play music for my class as they're coming into the classroom in the morning, something like Enya or Air. The kids call it "chill music". Instead of tumbling in, they come in quietly and there's a beautifully calm atmosphere for registration. I also use dance and drama quite a lot to make teaching more interesting. Quite recently, I used dance in science.

'On one occasion, all the kids were raindrops and evaporated from the sea, spiralled up to the clouds and ran back down through the rivers. We also did some work on the human heart where the children used blue and red sugar paper and took on the roles of the heart, the lungs and the blood within the context of an improvisational story about a giant. Everyone was involved and they're more likely to remember the workings of the heart through a piece of drama than if they'd been asked to draw a diagram from the board which would have bored them stupid. Active learning is always better than passive learning.

'I think if we're to improve children's experience at school, we need to pay far more attention to how they learn and adjust the curriculum to meet their specific needs. We also need less emphasis on results and more on developing children's social and life skills to help them become more fulfilled human beings. But, above all, we need to make learning much more fun and enjoyable for children and teachers!'

Elizabeth North is currently working as an advisory personal, social, health education teacher and has had twenty years experience of teaching PSHE, Food Technology and Textiles in the secondary sector.

'The fact that a child gets all of his input from his parents for four or five years proves just how important parenting is in our society. During those years, a child is wholly dependent on his parents for security, safety, self-expression and growth in all its forms. A huge part of parenting is imparting the joy of the world, the Wordsworthian idea that nature is a marvellous educator. Activities like playing with water, getting covered in mud, getting filthy dirty, are all parts of a child's early education. It's not about being indoors, sitting down and doing formal things, it's more important for young children to be outdoors, actively experiencing the natural environment. While I'm not in favour of formal lessons for very young children, I do think it's important for young children to experience the joy of books and to encourage them to listen to stories. Sharing a bedtime story is a vital form of readiness for reading and writing.

'While children need boundaries to work within to feel secure, discipline always needs to come from a loving place. I don't think smacking is ever any good for a child, although it might offer an emotional release for a parent! Once adults get to hitting they've lost it. They're doing what they tell a child not to. They're saying, "Because I can't think of anything else to do, I've just got to hurt you." I can understand how parents get to that point, because parenting often takes you to the absolute limits of your patience, but smacking simply doesn't work.

'In general, I don't think you can tell children things about the world, they have to experience them for themselves. When a child gets to 6 or 7, the parent has to start negotiating.

153

As they grow, children need to feel that their power and influence is becoming larger. They also have to learn to take on the responsibility of that power. It's a two-sided coin. Having choices carries responsibility. As a loving adult, if it all goes horribly wrong you have to let the children off the hook. You have to say, "That's fine, you're a child." You need to allow them the opportunity to pick up the pieces and start again. You can't bear grudges and hold things against children.

'Although I was loved in a rough-and-ready way, I was brought up with a rod of iron in an atmosphere of non-negotiation. I was furious at the time, which made me very rebellious as a child, and I still feel tremendously angry about that. I've worked on it through counselling. It was important for me to get my own views sorted out. Thankfully, a lot of my preparation for becoming a teacher focused on child studies, what being a parent is about, what being a carer of children is about. My particular course at Leeds Polytechnic was called teacher education rather than teacher training. It was strongly child-centred with a lot of emphasis on child psychology and developing the whole person. It's absolutely vital for student teachers to study these areas. I'm concerned that the one-year PGCE course for graduates, most of which is spent in schools on teaching practice, cannot possibly cover the type of child-centred issues that are vital for teaching.

'The ethos of a school is very important, especially on issues such as bullying. A child needs to know that if something goes wrong, they'll be listened to, taken seriously and the school will do all they can to do something about it. Schools also need to be aware of the way children are treated at breaks and lunchtimes and whether their views and opinions are valued through a school council. Other important areas of consideration are the way the day's structured, taking into account that children are little people who do not want to be shunted around, offering wider choice to pupils in terms of what they want to study, and the availability of a diverse range of social activities and clubs.

'It's things like these that make a child feel that "This is a good place to be, the adults care about me, have my interests at heart and look after me." There's currently a lot of talk about citizenship for schools and some people talk of it as watered-down politics. But done properly it's about setting up structures where children are listened to and feel empowered to make decisions. If children are given real responsibility and ownership of their school, they tend to get out of a school both what they want and need.

'I think there needs to be more emphasis on sex education in schools. It needs to be taught on a "little and often" basis and, in many schools, it needs to be introduced one or two years earlier. One of the schools I'm presently working at doesn't introduce sex education until year 10. This is far too late when you consider that young people are surrounded by sexual images from the media and music industry. They live in a world where sex is used to sell everything.

'Good sex education is about helping young people to get the best out of their experiences. Whatever teachers say, they're going to do it. It's our responsibility that we teach them to do it respectfully. Research shows that good sex education actually delays first experience by a couple of years. By helping children to examine both the fun side and the responsibility side, and talk about what it really means to be in a relationship, they are much more likely to make a considered judgement rather than act impulsively.

'Learning's not just about training for a job, it's about developing the whole person. I don't think there's enough emphasis on children's creativity in schools. For me, creativity is about nurturing an individual's response. It's not about just giving children things in terms of input, it's about giving licence and freedom to children to enable them to do things for themselves. This includes a specific vocabulary, confidence, a clear idea of what a specific subject, including the sciences, is for. We tend to forget that scientists are passionate people, too. They're not weirdos in white coats. Real science is about discovering the joys of the universe. But that's not what happens in schools, is it?

'As it is, children are being pushed through a sausage machine. It's a road we've gone down for so long in terms of everything having to be measured and outcomed, that I can't see us radically changing paths now. Being more accountable was a backlash against a lot of loose and foggy things that were going on. Teachers need to be accountable to a certain degree but I do think a creative teacher can work within that. I still think a teacher has a lot of autonomy and can make a difference to children's lives, not just academically but socially, spiritually and emotionally. I knew a young science teacher who was doing the business in terms of ticking the boxes but he was also letting off rockets in the classroom and teaching circus skills after school!

'When young people look back on their school days, they remember enthusiasm from people more than subjects, teachers who were on their side. They also remember the nasty stuff, teachers who treated them unkindly and unfairly. Other things that stay with them are sports activities, concerts and plays, and the knowledge that they achieved something academically. But, above all, they remember their friends. The social interaction that goes on amongst children is the most important element of their school lives. It helps children to know who they are and how to relate to the world. Education for young people is about getting the best they can out of what life's got on offer and encouraging the sort of attitudes and skills that equip them to be able to go on and learn effectively for themselves and to interact with others. It's also about developing a value system which they can draw upon when needs be.'

Lynne Jackson is a classroom assistant in the modern language department in a secondary school. She has a degree in psychology and is a sports enthusiast, having played county tennis and badminton. She lived in France for 17 years and is an interpreter in French. She is a lone parent with a 16-year-old daughter and a 14-year-old son.

'The role of a classroom assistant is often underestimated in terms of a support for the teacher and children. A well-motivated classroom assistant can offer academic, social and psychological support. They can target specific individuals with behavioural problems, high-flyers, underachievers, those who are not getting enough attention as well as pupils who may need emotional support. With the ultimate aim of encouraging all children to participate in the lesson, an assistant's specific support and praise for small efforts made by disruptive children or low achievers can do quite a lot to raise the ethos of a class. There is also a counselling element to the job, e.g. if a child is withdrawn or refusing to work, the assistant might be able to offer a listening ear, a sympathetic voice, an opportunity to share a problem. All this support leaves the teacher free to concentrate on the overall lesson.

'Having a boy and a girl myself, I see a difference in how they respond to learning and life. Boys and girls seem to be genetically programmed to act and respond in quite distinct ways. Boys are certainly a lot more active. In class, they have a tendency to pencil-bang, foot-tap and turn around. I'm convinced that this more active mode of behaviour is not deliberate but an innate need to be free of physical constraint and restraint after a certain time. Boys, in particular, need a physical outlet, a channel for their considerable energies. Girls, on the other hand, seem more suited to structure, conformity and concentration.

'Young people can only take so much mental input before

they seek physical release. There needs to be a daily opportunity for physical education, whether it be dance, movement, gymnastics or sport. Plenty of fresh air and exercise are vital for kids. I know from being involved in a lot of sport myself, there is a definite physical and psychological feel-good factor about it. I'm sure that once children have had the opportunity to oxygenate their brains, they are more likely to settle into a formal lesson and exhibit less volatile behaviour in the classroom.

'The right kind of ambience in a classroom is very important if a child is to give of their best. Teachers and classroom assistants have to be conscious of their mode of communication, how they are delivering and what kids are receiving. The tone of your voice, the choice of words and the manner in which you communicate with children are very important. They don't like to be spoken at or down to, patronised or shouted at, which is only reasonable. Before they've even sat down in their places, children can sometimes feel aggressed by the lack of respect for their person.

'Young people have a very acute sense of fair play and resent not being treated fairly in the classroom. Even when they're not doing what's expected of them at a particular moment in time, they need to feel valued as individuals. It needs to be conveyed to all children that they are intrinsically good and acceptable, even if their behaviour at a given time is not acceptable.

'We need to appreciate that many children are anti-school for all sorts of reasons and often struggle just to get there in the morning, not least because they fail to see the link between the daily grind of lessons and their personal future. The last thing they need at school is antagonism and confrontation. This is especially true of adolescents, who find the transition from childhood to adulthood painful and bewildering. Teenagers need a solid, reliable presence, someone to listen to them, empathise with and understand their problems. Even when their behaviour is obnoxious, they still need understanding and a little bit of TLC!'

Helen Buchanan is head teacher of St Clement's Church of England Primary School on the Ordsall estate in Salford. This school's intake is one of Britain's poorest, where 50% of the children have special needs and 90% have free school meals.

'Since the right kind of parenting is absolutely crucial to a child's emotional development, any parent who cannot cope with the demands of the job needs to be offered immediate help. I am lucky enough to have secured an outreach clinic from the children's hospital, which is run by a child mental health worker. There is also support from a clinical psychologist, and parents volunteer themselves when they feel they cannot cope with their children's behaviour. It's the only pilot of its kind in the Northwest and sessions are available during the school day.

'I would like to see all schools like mine getting multi-agency workers in school for families. I believe if you support the parents, you support the children. In an ideal world, the school nurse needs to visit weekly, parents need to have access to a child mental health worker at their local primary school, learning mentors need to bridge the gap between home and school for reluctant attenders and an educational psychologist needs to be a practitioner as well as an assessor for the statementing process.

'My staff recognise that a lot of our children come in to school at three years of age having had very little intellectual or emotional stimulation, which results in limited curiosity and few skills. They have been dumbed down by a diet of TV and noise pollution and have experienced limited interaction with their parents, which results in difficulties with selective listening. Half of the children entering nursery have speech and language difficulties, often caused by continuous ear infections in infancy. Also prevalent are asthma and attention deficit disorder. Sadly, many of our

160

intake seem to have given up on learning through play due to constant chastisement – "Don't touch!", "Shut up!", etc.

'We employ a learning mentor, who spends a great deal of time listening to children talk about their feelings. They liaise with teachers, keeping them informed about potential bullying issues. The mentor attends the junior youth club to ensure that she mixes with all the children, not just those with issues. Bullying is a serious issue in today's schools.

'We maintain strict vigilance and procedures to ensure that the children know that we have zero tolerance in this matter. I am convinced that bullying has increased in schools because society has approved and condoned name-calling on the radio and TV. The "alternative" comedy programmes of the 1980s and 90s were often based on humiliation and name-calling for cheap laughs at the expense of others.

'We also live in a highly competitive society which has manifested itself in schools through the league tables. I would like to see league tables based purely on value-added point scoring, which Ofsted already use to measure progress. The whole notion of assessing and judging, which has grown out of the national tests, is crippling children's spirits and creativity. Schools need to maintain a risk-free, have-a-go environment to avoid turning children into objects of appraisal and judgement. The child has become a means to an end, where the main aim is to get a result. It takes a strong leader to fight these short-term indicators at the expense of long-term gains which encourage self-motivation.

'At our school, we have quite a few well-informed strategies to help children develop their individuality. They include an accelerated learning programme, fostering emotional intelligence, quality religious education, breakfast clubs and out-of-school activities. Our assemblies have moments of silence and we teach children the power of prayer and kind thoughts. We consider the school ethos needs to include teaching manners, as this promotes tolerance and empathy. We have developed judo sessions in the school day to develop self-discipline and self-control, and we use drama, play therapy and role play to enrich children's emotional well-being. Although the arts have been marginalised by the core subjects, I fight to bring more music, dance, drama and visual arts into the curriculum. It's my belief that the arts are what make human beings human beings and distinguish us from apes!

'Out-of-school and lunchtime activities are extremely underrated as a powerful tool of a broader view of education. They need to be used creatively and help nurture a democratic system where the children feel unconditionally valued. Teachers who run clubs develop quality relationships that often shed light on a child in a way lessons don't.

'Even if a child has been excluded from a class for disruptive behaviour, no one is excluded from after-school clubs. We believe this is a way of healing relationships before the next day so that a child will not become disaffected.

'Our society has tended to nurture female and male stereotypes, which impacts the way children perform at school. Girls are still groomed as potential Barbie dolls or wrapped in cotton wool and treated like gold dust. Girls not only look more vulnerable, they have also benefited from the equal opportunities drive. Boys get the hard reality of "If he hits you, hit him back," and the employment images of the 21st century have not helped less academic boys who once had greater opportunities as apprentice engineers or mechanics. Boys have always been late developers, but now they are less likely to catch up later on. They get easily demotivated by girls' early success.

'Society has also become more immature, encouraging fast-pace living and calling for faster responses. All this is sweeping our children along in a culture that does not encourage reflection or a "stop and think before you act" mentality. Modern life is so fast that nobody has time to

162

talk to a child these days and our society is the poorer for it. The technological revolution has started to show a downside. Just as the industrial revolution was the catalyst to the introduction of the state school system, the technological revolution will force the education system to be redefined once more – hopefully sooner rather than later. Schools can no longer be modelled on the academic institutions of the past. Schools are now the guardians of the future emotional well-being of our nation!'

Angela Mills is head teacher at Meridian C.P. School, Peacehaven, East Sussex. She has also been a foster parent to 17 children.

'If you read the first published document on the National Curriculum (1988), it clearly states: "At the heart of the school is the curriculum." Contrast this with both the "Hadow Report" (1933) and, thirty years later, the "Plowden Report" (1967) on children and their primary schools, which place the child at the heart of the school. In all my years of teaching, I've never faltered from my philosophy that the child is the most important part of education. I may be regarded as anarchic, subversive, even revolutionary, but above all I'm incredibly into creativity.

'Everyone's a creative being and the need to express creatively is absolutely inherent in a child. I say to the children at our school, "You are all brilliant and gorgeous and you mustn't hide your light. God has given you all a precious gift and your journey through life is to find your gift. You may already know what it is, you may not find it for a while, but you've all got a gift."

'Children aren't empty pots that we have to stuff things into. They're abundantly overflowing with lots of talents and abilities. It's our job as teachers to draw things out and help children discover themselves. Being a teacher is an amazing privilege. I never forget that. I'm privileged to have the parents' trust and to work with children on the first part of their journey through life. It's important to remember that a child is a parent's greatest treasure, and even if they have difficulties they must never be demeaned.

'When the children come in to school in the morning, they are each given an individual welcome from their teacher – "How are you today?", which is followed by an uplifting comment such as "We're going to have a wonderful day together." There is music playing and toys and games set

164

out to help put them at their ease. At assembly, some people may think I've lost it, but I tell the children that they're very special, bright shiny souls, and hope that they will have an amazing day and live their dreams. I'm not afraid to say to a child, "I love you". I don't want to say it to their tombstone, I need to say it now. Visitors are amazed when children give me a kiss or a hug.

'From the age of eight, each child has a notebook that they keep to record their ambitions, goals and dreams. One of our ten-year-old pupils has severe learning problems but he has no difficulty with whole-body movements and his goal is to climb the Himalayas. We go on the Internet together and he prints off pictures and information that will help him realise his dream. He knows he is going to need a lot of equipment and he is determined to write down everything he will need for his journey. By tapping into his passion, he recently gained two years on a reading test.

'Because we're interested in the individuality of each child, we're interested in how each of them learns. We try to go along with their preferred learning style because all children have unique types and levels of intelligence. Most people are visual learners but teachers are often auditory learners, with a tendency toward logic and left-brain thinking. We make sure that our children have a lot of exposure to visual and creative experiences to develop the artistic right side of the brain, too. We bring in creative artists and do a lot of work on feelings, emotions and self-expression.

'It's also important to look at children's kinaesthetic, whole-body learning. When we are teaching little children to write, we don't ask them to put pen to paper straightaway. They are given two terms of whole-body movements, which involve games using circles, zigzags, colours and shapes. They make marks on big paper using big fat pens. Once the whole body is coordinated, they are then ready to start working on the fine motor skills necessary for writing.

'In an effort to always focus on the learner, our teachers come up with all sorts of innovative ways of presenting things, e.g. one teacher has been talking about character in a story with a class of 6–7-year-olds. She took the book *Burglar Bill* and made a bag of swag containing all the things he'd stolen. She'd also drawn and painted a picture of Bill, and the children were invited to describe what he looked like – stripy jumper, holding a cat, etc. It just so happened that in assembly we'd been focusing on the subject of not judging people by their appearance and looking at such issues as "How do you know what somebody's really like?"

'The teacher pointed out that while Burglar Bill has stubble on his chin and looks fierce, it is also important to know how he strokes his cat, because this would help us to know the real Burglar Bill!

'To help develop listening skills, we use a sequence of hand movements. We ask the children to place their palms on their cheeks, pointing toward their eyes to signify that they are watching; to touch their ears to make sure they are listening; to place one hand on their foreheads to show that they are thinking and, finally, to put one palm on their hearts to indicate that they are feeling. This routine, which embraces the senses, the mind and the heart, alerts the children to the fact that the teacher may want a response from them on any of these levels.

'One of our most recent initiatives is to help our children think philosophically by forming a community of enquiry. So many adults laugh [at] or trivialise children's thoughts and questions, but we aim to value them. We'll take a story like *Where The Wild Things Are* or *Not Now, Bernard* and the children will pose questions about what they've read, e.g. "Is it a dream?", "What makes us real?" [or] "If I leave the room do I still exist?" This kind of line of enquiry really engages children.

'In order to encourage these kind of activities, it's important for teachers to think outside the box and to be brave enough to get off their knees and say what they believe in. Our staff do a lot of work on emotional intelligence, e.g. learning to trust themselves a bit more so that they can develop greater trust in their pupils. It's also vital that teachers feel valued. How else can they value the children? I encourage my staff to speak up if something's going wrong. If they're angry about something they are encouraged to express it. If a member of staff is having relationship problems, or stressed out from the job, they are advised to go home and get their heads and hearts straight. This kind of open communication, which visiting students can find quite daunting, actually results in very little staff absence. My vision is to see teachers working with the children for four days and having one day a week non-contact time.

'Staff are encouraged to go out at break times to play with the children. We need to consider what kind of message we're giving to children when we turn them out onto a bleak expanse of tarmac on a cold winter's day while staff are warm and cosy inside drinking a cup of coffee.

'The children feel abandoned and left wondering why. Play time is a very important part of a child's day, and they enjoy sharing it with adults. We have three sheds of play equipment and have themed weeks such as a skipping week, a bat and ball week or a parachute week. We also tend not to watch the clock, e.g. if it's snowing, we allow the children to go out on a spur-of-the-moment basis and enjoy it!

'We aim to empower the children by giving them an opportunity to express their opinions through a school council. Much of the quality of feeling and debate amongst the children would put the House of Commons to shame! Their recent agenda has included quizzing the cook about why there are no seconds at lunchtime, asking the chair of governors about the allocation of funds for their own budget to buy a water fountain and more playground toys, and to collaborate with the teachers on helping to improve the school environment, and the setting up of a "buddy system" in the playground, so that every child is paired up and no one is left feeling alone.'

Peter Sharp is a Principal Consultant for Mouchel Parkman plc and was formerly principal educational psychologist for Southampton City Council and chair of the National Emotional Literacy Interests Group (NELIG). He now works mainly at a strategic level with LEAs across the country. He and his wife, Lindsay, have two young children, aged 14 and 13.

'My thinking on integrating social and emotional development work into the curriculum was influenced by Daniel Goleman's 1996 best-seller *Emotional Intelligence*. He put forward the idea that the ability to recognise, understand and handle emotions is as important as the hypothetico-deductive intellectual processes that can be measured. In its widest context, emotional literacy can help to promote creativity, innovation and leadership while, for school children, it basically translates as "to feel good equals to learn good".

'For several years, I'd been feeling there was a need to put the heart back into the curriculum. I kept telling myself that we needed to go through the grimness to get to the truth. The child-centred approach of the sixties had sown some positive seeds but it lacked rigour, and in the seventies there was a cultural awareness that relationships were the fourth "R". But nothing could prevent the education system of the latter part of the twentieth century becoming a sausage machine which churned out clones and measured success by material acquisition. We also saw all young people being force-fed on a curriculum of GCSEs when they were never designed for all pupils.

'There were a vast number of children feeling emotionally bereft and ill-served by a system that placed so much emphasis only on academic achievement. It was becoming increasingly important to help pupils access their emotions to help them deal with all sorts of alienating factors both inside and outside the education system. Of course, for this to happen teachers need to be in touch with their emotions and adept at handling the social dynamics of a classroom. One of my greatest concerns is that many PGCE courses for teachers have stripped out the psychology component in favour of competency-based training. This means that you can now qualify as a teacher without studying child psychology and with no real understanding of group dynamics.

"The opportunity to bring emotional literacy into Southampton's schools was realised when the city became a unitary authority in 1997. Because we had no baggage, we became a "can do" LEA. The chief inspector had also read Goleman's book and, with his support together with the director and other managers, we became the first local education authority to introduce a citywide emotional literacy curriculum. In the past few years, we have piloted programmes in schools across the whole city, placing emotional literacy alongside literacy and numeracy as the primary aims of a strategic education plan. Now all ninety schools are involved in what has become a self-sustaining project. Southampton continues to place Emotional Literacy at the heart of its Education Development Plan.

'In the early stages, we piloted a programme on anger management in an attempt to reduce the level of permanent exclusions in the city's schools. Now, on a much wider scale, through seminars, workshops, presentations and publications, Southampton is developing an emotional literacy curriculum with a diverse content. It includes conscious awareness to help children build a feelings vocabulary. When pupils arrive at some of our schools, we find that they have a feeling vocabulary of only up to ten words. When emotional literacy is introduced, it equips pupils with more appropriate words and responses. Our strategy is also designed to help children understand their thoughts, feelings and actions so as to permit informed decision making; managing feelings so as to be more effective in getting needs met without isolating the interests of others as well as promoting self-

170

esteem, managing conflict, understanding the dynamics of groups and developing communication skills.

'SELIG (Southampton Emotional Literacy Interest Group) led to the development of an online network and cyberforum for people to share information and ideas (www.nelig.com.). There is now also WELIG (in Wiltshire), DELIG (in Dumbartonshire) and NELIG, the national network and service, which aims to promote emotional intelligence at a societal level. It is a strategy that can just as easily be applied to trade and industry as it can to prisons. There are several new Emotional Literacy Interest groups ('Eligs') and more about to be formed.

'Mason Moor Primary is just one of the schools in Southampton where an holistic approach to emotional literacy is already helping to give children the kind of life skills they need to relate to others and with themselves, at school and beyond. Former head teacher Sue Nicholson claimed that it has helped reduce playground violence and raised the standard of work generally, including the Literacy Hour. She is aware that while it may not be possible to cure social problems, it can build up pupils' resilience and communication skills, which not only help them to cope more easily with problems in school but also with domestic conflicts.

'Education chiefs in Southampton were delighted when Ofsted inspectors commented that the emotional literacy strategy is "highly valued by the project schools and is contributing to improved levels of behaviour management in schools". This gives the green light to other LEAs to implement their own strategies. There is also a lot of interest from central government, the DfES, the DTI and the Home Office. Emotional literacy is topical and current. It is definitely an idea whose time has come.'

Peter Abbs is Professor of Creative Writing at the University of Sussex He is also a poet and arts educator committed to a new metaphysical poetics and a new paradigm for arts education. He has published six volumes of poetry and many books on aesthetic education. He has lectured and given readings in Europe, Australia, India and the USA.

' "Aesthetic" is not a word people use with comfort and when they do they're not quite sure what they mean by it. My aim is to clarify the word and to make it a crucial concept in arts education. While aesthetic experience cannot be put into logical concepts or a precise philosophical formulation, it does include a strong element of cognition involving knowing and understanding of the world. Of course, we generally think of knowing and understanding as conceptual in nature, and that's where the problem lies.

'A lot of people say if you can't fully explain it, if you can't quantify it and you can't logically formulate it, it's subjective and private, and then it gets categorised as something that's not very significant. What one is doing in defending the aesthetic is defending a particular sensuous and imaginal form of understanding which, like all forms of knowledge, is essentially communal in nature and concerns the whole of civilisation.

'It's this lack of significant experience that's missing in our schools. I'm concerned for the fate of thousands of children in our culture whose aesthetic mode of intelligence goes often unrecognised and, where recognised, undervalued and unfulfilled. While children are innately creative, the education system is stifling and the arts they are being exposed to are often totally incoherent. The arts are mis-understood by 90% of people in our society, even in the teaching profession, and that ignorance makes me feel evangelical about it.

'As conventional religious belief declines, the place of

172

aesthetic experience is even more important. Aesthetic experience, through the arts, opens the ethical and spiritual dimension of human life. For example, *The Magic Flute* concerns spiritual meaning, levels of being. As conventional religions die the arts should move in and serve as great agents elaborating the metaphysical and spiritual. That has, also, been their main traditional function, of course.

'Looking at the aesthetic from a global perspective, I believe it can be an imaginative power for engendering understanding. Rites, rituals, music, poetry, dance, narrative, nursery rhymes – all exist to kindle a sense of human solidarity. If society is to rekindle a common symbolic purpose, its children must have sustained aesthetic experience and it is never too early to start.

'Story-time is an example of how a reception teacher might introduce aesthetic experience. Just sitting quietly and attending to narrative through the imagination is an experience that is absolutely crucial. If the following day that story is used as the basis for drama work then the children are getting an experience of narrative and drama which can later be connected to other art forms: to music, ceramics, dance and so forth.

'It's perfectly possible to introduce a class of young children to Shakespeare – it's not what you do, it's how you do it! If you do it badly, then you can do a lot of harm but if you can introduce *Hamlet* to young children in a sensitive way – say, taking the ghost scene with seven-year-olds – it's prefiguring what will come later and taking the child creatively into his or her cultural inheritance.

'For the pressurised teacher who complains that there is not enough time for the arts in an already over-crowded curriculum, teachers have got to be convinced that what we call the aesthetic dimension is crucially important in education. The head teacher, who is responsible for shaping the curriculum, has to be persuaded by it. If a head invites creative artists into school, then that sets the standard. It's also important to involve the community. By bringing parents in to watch a great play or hear a performance of good music, you're not only educating your pupils but also the community.

'I'm not too optimistic about the future of the arts in our state schools. The National Curriculum has mechanised the curriculum and destroyed the creative spirit of teaching. As I have argued in my most recent work, "Against The Flow: Education, The Arts and Postmodern Culture" (Routledge, Falmer, 2003) what is required is a revolution! We need to return to the notions of creative pedagogy, to the notions of inspired teaching, to animating the best of our culture in relationship to the imagination of the child. It is not going to be easy but the very quality and meaning of our life is in the balance. There has to be a swing against the current educational oppression. Perhaps it is already beginning.'

Ted Wragg is Emeritus Professor of Education at Exeter University, author of over 50 books on education as well as a frequent radio and TV broadcaster.

'I believe young people are buried by a routine of sameness and need to discover themselves. I'm talking about the 11–14 age range who are buried under a uniform curriculum; having to endure a constant, rigid diet of 13 subjects (including citizenship, introduced in 2002), which are delivered one after the other. At this stage of their education, adolescents have reached physical maturity, adult size, and yet they are still being given a top primary school type of education with no choices.

'Every school should be staffed and resourced to give every individual the advice and support they need as well as a curriculum that challenges the intellect and the imagination. This involves a coherent programme which will help young people to discover who they are and how they can fulfil themselves as individuals. As it is, adolescents carry with them a sense of abandonment. Although it is part of their birthright to be offered a rite of passage into society, we are doing little to nurture their aspirations and hopes for the future. It's no wonder that they turn to a fag or alcohol for consolation.

'I was certainly in favour of the general principles of the National Curriculum, but its contents have filled up the week to such an extent that we've lost the type of flexibility that gave adolescents who were non-examination candidates the opportunity to excel. Testing is a particularly hard part of our education system and some aspects of the National Curriculum can be quite repressive. For instance, while I'm in favour of the Literacy Hour, I'm against how the teacher is specifically directed to split it up. The notion of "one size fits all" works against the principle of flexibility. It's my belief that all children deserve an entitlement of great flexibility which transcends being rich or poor, living north or south.

'At the moment, the learning experience for adolescents tends to be disjointed. The bell goes and everyone changes subject. There needs to be greater autonomy for schools to suspend the timetable for certain weeks of the year and to extend some lessons. When you think about it, adult lives are not a series of hourlong projects. It's much more about sustained effort, which is sometimes needed for days or weeks at a time.

'Fortunately, there are schools that are breaking away from this approach, which has proved a fine servant but a cruel master. For instance, Stantonbury High School in Milton Keynes, which has performing arts status, is trying to dispense with a lesson-a-day approach to timetabling. They've got 100 pupils doing GCSE music and a wide range of all the other arts.

'I think the performing arts do a great deal for children. The opportunity to study a script, rehearse and perform, is an incredibly valuable growing experience. In fact, I'd go as far as to say that young people who miss out on these kinds of experiences are diminished as citizens and lose out on their democratic rights. I know from my own education how much music and drama meant to me as a child. I can remember large chunks of my music lessons, a choir of 100 and an orchestra of 70. It was all down to my music teacher, Norman Barnes, who had enormous enthusiasm for his subject. His classes were always a bit unruly and I'm sure that he would have failed to meet all the criteria that Ofsted now demand, but he was proof that no one forgets a good teacher. In his case, where one bright light was extinguished, hundreds burn on in its place.

'Then there was the opportunity to play the Second Witch in *Macbeth*. Not only did I know my own part, I knew the whole play by heart and could have understudied for anyone else. This was followed by Brutus in *Julius Caesar*. I'm sure that by learning his 700 lines and having to deal with the angst of what I should do about Julius Caesar gave me tremendous opportunities for reflection and nurtured a self-belief. Confidence is a matter of practice. It was experiences like these that later enabled me to address 5,000 people at the Royal Albert Hall and millions of viewers on television.

'Another area of the curriculum that we need to look at is the strong premium placed on language, which is geared to the reading and writing of exam questions, while subjects which involve making and doing, intelligent action, are downgraded to a lesser status. While highly valued in Germany and the USA, we dismiss an intuitive understanding of how to mend things as being "good with your hands".

'At any stage of their learning, a child is only as good a learner as their emotional stability allows. I undertook a study of literacy which focused on levels of improvement in an academic year. One girl, who had received a lot of support from her mother in writing an extended story, showed a massive gain of 33 points in a reading test, while a boy whose parents were splitting up and [who had] lapsed into a dreamlike state dropped 25 points in the same test. Here were two children in the same class, taught by the same teacher, exhibiting polarised responses to their emotional state at a given time.

'Bertrand Russell described the aim of education as "freedom". Education, if done properly, should allow an individual freedom to read, travel, participate in a democratic society, to be aware of rights and obligations. For all this to happen, schools need to offer a greater diversity, allowing pupils an opportunity to nurture their individuality, an ability to think for themselves and a greater understanding of their role as a member of society. Of course, conformity and orderliness are important parts of life, but we also need diversity, which is nurtured when we allow children to think for themselves. Dissent, the unusual, the unpredictable, the imaginative are the driving forces in a healthy society.'

Alistair Smith is founder of Alite (Accelerated Learning in Training and Education). He has written six books and has been described as 'the country's leading trainer in modern learning methods'.

' "Accelerated Learning" is an umbrella term for a series of practical approaches to learning which benefit from new knowledge about how the brain functions; motivation and self-belief; accessing different sorts of intelligence and retaining and recalling information. Accelerated Learning carries with it the expectation that, when properly motivated and appropriately taught, all learners can reach a level of achievement which currently may seem beyond them. The main aim of the seven-point accelerated learning cycle, in relation to teaching in the classroom, is that students learn to learn and thus gain lifelong learning skills.

'Increasingly, it is recognised that self-belief, self-esteem and motivation influence performance in the classroom. Classrooms characterised by uncertainty and risk, frequent put-down and rare praise are classrooms where purposeful learning does not take place. Sometimes, teachers struggle to remain positive and don't recognise that their own self-esteem needs working on. In my experience, there are some teachers who actually don't like teaching and don't like children. This may stem from them not liking themselves. This is not as surprising as it may sound, because teachers are a cross section of society and they therefore experience similar challenges to the rest of us as we all struggle to improve our relationships with children and ourselves.

'In order for teachers to help their pupils learn, they have to be learners themselves. I try to provide teachers with a model for self-esteem which will help them to be more positive about who they are and what they're doing. This approach is designed with the ultimate aim of improving student motivation and raising achievement in all ability levels. The BASICS model that I use embraces some of the many and varied programmes which exist in the UK and the USA, aimed at building self-esteem in adults and children.

'The acronym starts with B, which is for "belonging" because we all need to feel approved and respected by others. A is for "aspirations", because a learner needs to believe that learning has some purpose. S is for "safety", involving a strong sense of feeling comfortable and safe within a group, where the expectations and ground rules are known and accepted. I is for "identity", meaning that the learner has knowledge of their own strengths and weaknesses, values and beliefs. C is for "challenge". The final S is for "success", because regular and positive affirmation of success – however large or small – reinforces the belief that the learner has control over his or her own life.

'Many of today's children are cosseted – dropped off and picked up from school by car and then put in front of a television or computer game. They are often missing out on circumstances which put them at moderate risk, which were more readily available to the previous generation, e.g. opportunities for explorative play. In addition, much of the present school system encourages conformity, where pupils are judged by what they know, and success is measured by replicating information on paper.

'We need to be less obsessive about formal education and provide a wider variety of experience in schools. This includes offering language-rich, multi-sensory, holistic environments for children which afford exposure to a wide range of the arts. The arts in schools are important, because they offer life situations in very safe circumstances, and cannot be introduced early enough. It is also vitally important to provide more opportunities for children to release pent-up energy through more physical activity. Lessons could be broken up by more physical breaks – even if they're no longer than 40 seconds – to allow children to move around and alter their mood and mindset before they resume tasks which involve focus and application.

'One of the most alienating aspects of the education system is its tendency to be more girl-friendly. Girls lean towards being conscientious, neat, considered and precise, while boys tend to be natural speculators and risk takers and are often more tactile. The fact that the curriculum is delivered in a way that is all too formal, and too early, doesn't always sit well with boys and often berates them before they've barely got started. In such circumstances, they can develop an early aversion to school, especially to reading and writing.

'To redress the imbalance, boys need visual, auditory and kinaesthetic (VAK) input. A classroom of learners will include some who are visual learners, some who are auditory learners and some who are kinaesthetic learners. To avoid teaching their own preferred system most or all of the time, teachers need to have a repertoire of strategies which embrace all three types of learners. Without this kind of input, communication is largely with one group, leaving the other two groups feeling excluded.

'In my early books, I discussed the concept of multi-intelligences as defined by Howard Gardner, the idea that intelligence is not a fixed entity concerning only cognition, but multiple – embracing mathematical, linguistic, visual and spatial, musical, kinaesthetic, naturalist as well as interpersonal and intrapersonal skills. Gardner believes that, while we are all born with multiple intelligences, each individual will have different strengths and weaknesses and, in many ways, these determine how easy it is for a person to learn information when it is presented in a particular way.

'Most learners will have a "jagged" profile, which means that while they could be excellent in one area, they might be weak in another, e.g. a gifted sportsman, musician or artist might have a restricted view in some areas of learning, but have the capability to be highly regarded in a particular field and make a great deal of money from their expertise or flair. We all have preferred styles of learning and, for effective learning to take place, teachers not only have to cater for these styles and different modes of learning in the classroom but also know how to assess them. The question is no longer "How intelligent are you?", but "In what ways are you intelligent?"'

James Park is the director and co-founder of Antidote ('the organisation that promotes emotional literacy'). He is a psychotherapist and author of several books, including Sons, Mothers and Other Lovers.

'Our education system undervalues social and collaborative learning. This was well captured by a management consultant friend of mine who said, "The quality we most value in business is what we would call 'cheating' in schools." He meant that schools place too much emphasis on individual endeavour and not nearly enough on cooperation, allowing children to work in groups and to tackle problems together. We need to nurture a greater sense of self as a way of fostering collaboration. We live in a culture which misunderstands the relationship between self and group. We tend to think that if you develop self then you become less able to engage with a group. The opposite is actually more accurate.

'One of the problems with the emotional intelligence movement is that too often it's seen as a technique for individuals to gain an advantage and reach the top of the ladder. But how emotionally literate we might be within one organisation may differ from how emotionally literate we might be within another. What's important is how the organisation affects us. A colleague of mine was describing the different emotional responses he had to two schools. He found on entering one that he felt "deranged" by the frenetic atmosphere. He found the ambience of the other quite calming, even though he'd just had a row with his wife!

'It is important that all young people are given opportunities for dialogue. By that, I mean an active process of sharing perspectives and possibilities which enhance the learning experience. Dialogue is a particularly effective way to learn because it engages young people emotionally at the same time as it stimulates their thinking. It also promotes self-confidence and well-being in pupils and teachers. Dialogue has the potential to contribute to the study of every curriculum subject. It involves a commitment on the part of those involved to appreciate the thoughts, feelings and values of others.

'Emotional literacy needs to be approached in an holistic way, in terms of the whole community. Within schools, staff, pupils, parents and the wider community all need to be involved. Schools are one of the last community institutions and I think good schools think through their relationships with all the school members and the larger community. On the other hand, some schools get into a blaming culture when things go wrong, where teachers blame parents and parents blame teachers. They need to get to a point where they can acknowledge and activate their common interests rather than focusing on their differences.

'One of the problems with our culture is that we meet a lot of people that we don't know. We need to create situations where people can interact in emotional safety, so that they are not always on their guard or defensive, to get out of a pattern of concealment and closure. We also need to develop situations where people can learn to trust each other. In regard to the classroom, by focusing on individual competition and measuring that performance we do too little about enabling young people to trust and support each other. What we're talking about are situations where people's anxieties are left unresolved and [are] possibly accentuated, rather than situations where the sources of their anxiety are being addressed. By working collaboratively, all sorts of richnesses are nurtured that support intuitive and creative learning.

'I had an education where I performed well intellectually but was less successful in developing a broad range of skills. There's certainly a place for academic excellence in schools, but it shouldn't be at the expense of emotional and social development. School is a social space. If teachers and governors don't look after that social environment they are not maximising its potential. There need to be all sorts of opportunities for children to develop skills other than the intellectual. It is only by becoming emotionally literate that young people can liberate their creativity, adaptability, resourcefulness and resilience. Another great advantage of accessing your emotions is that it gives you the ability to think clearly under pressure when faced with difficult and challenging tasks.

'Considering how disempowered children are in British schools, I'm amazed that most turn up every day. There needs to be far more dialogue between teachers and pupils so that young people feel more valued and less dumped upon. Children need more input into shaping and delivering the curriculum and greater freedom to respond to what's being asked of them. What excites me is when teachers teach in a way that responds to the needs and interests of children rather than focusing on delivery and achievement of certain skills. This works both ways. Teachers also need to feel empowered. I think something as prescriptive as the Literacy Hour is not always a very effective way to empower teachers.

'Whatever the content of the lesson, teaching's about making a connection with children. There seems to be a belief that if you keep pouring things into kids they'll eventually find a connection. Surely this is starting things from the wrong place. It is crazy to start from the basis that there is a body of knowledge here and it's the teacher's responsibility to transmit it to pupils over there. That creates enormous strain for a teacher and it doesn't use the greatest classroom resource – the children's curiosity and the opportunity for pupils to start from what they're interested in. Children not only need the means to process the information they already have but to find ways to get to the information they need to develop their curiosity and learning skills. I'm

185

in agreement with people who say that we've gone from a culture which is relationship-rich and information-poor to a culture which is information-rich and relationship-poor. Children don't remember information studied in actual lessons. What stays with them is the relationships they formed. They remember the teachers who are positive, loving, relating and connecting.

'One of the functions of Antidote is to collect evidence about how emotional literacy impacts all areas of our society. A story that really struck home to me came out of a recent collaboration with the library service and the youth service. A group of youths were composing rap songs and had been really frustrated because they needed a broader repertoire of rhymes. It was only through their contact with the library service that they discovered the existence of rhyming dictionaries. It's a rather sad reflection on our education system that they had never been given the resources at school to develop their creativity.'

Lea Misan is managing director of Heartskills, which works in the home, the workplace, the school and the community to 'foster the social, emotional development of individuals by helping them learn to connect, value and harness feelings positively; think critically and creatively; make responsible choices and take meaningful action'. She is also a writer, lawyer and mother of three children.

'Parents are the first educators of children. As young people mature, other adults and peers contribute to children's development, but it is the emotional–behavioural patterns and habits of parents which are most likely to be mirrored by their offspring. Parents' attitudes and efforts determine how a child resolves the conflicting messages of the home and the wider community. Caring parents provide an anchor, a reference point for their children, including [a model of] the kind of parent they will one day become.

'I believe that there are two broad purposes of education. The first is to provide children with a framework, a common body of knowledge and/or rules that will enable them to live, work and play cooperatively with one another. The second is to develop children's emotional lives, which helps to build character. Character building requires a degree of self-knowledge which can only be acquired through emotional and social development.

'I don't think it's possible to raise academic standards by disregarding the social and emotional well-being of children. If we focus our attention on the lack or shortfall of academic achievement, we are sure to attract just that. Instead, we need to focus on the enabling factors, the learning environment, the confidence and self-esteem of our children. The "fun factor" is also an integral part of learning. A love of learning can only be acquired by tapping into children's emotions.

'Language and the arts provide the building blocks of emotional literacy. They enable the expression of feelings

187

without which there can be little or no self-awareness. The handling of emotions has little value if it is not accompanied by the ability to express one's feelings and tap into the information feelings provide to determine behavioural options. To nurture a more aesthetic approach to learning in schools, we need to integrate a wide variety of opportunities for artistic enhancement, e.g. school excursions to art museums, inviting artists into schools.

'We need to dispense with the "this is how I will know that children have learnt x approach" and adopt a more autonomous method that enables young people to explore themselves and their environment at their own pace. Adults need to be more attuned to children's learning styles, have the ability to let go of their own agendas concerning children and provide more structure and opportunities for their guided discovery through self-awareness. For teachers to encourage self-reflection in children, they need to be more in touch with their own emotional lives and nurture an ability to create time and space for their own personal self-reflection. They also need to be able to resolve conflict amongst themselves, and with the system in which they work, in as many empowering and creative ways as possible.

'In general, I think there's too much competition in schools. It's due to a paradigm from which we are fortunately now shifting, but it still permeates our society. The difficulty is achieving the right balance between healthy competition, which we still need today, and collaboration, which we increasingly need and upon which our children will most certainly depend. We need to develop activities and games that encourage collaboration and reduce the emphasis on tests, which are more for the convenience of teachers than helping children to learn. In our eagerness to decrease competition, it is important that it does not disappear entirely as it, too, has its role to play in the emotional development of children.

'For those children who exhibit behavioural problems at school, the first step to helping them is to assess whether such behaviour is reflecting a parent's or teacher's perspective and/or behaviour. Once that's been established, teachers can employ quite a few strategies to help children with challenging behaviour. They can listen to a child's personal and learning needs. They can examine their own teaching methods. They can then consider a different learning style to match the specific needs of the child. I'm reminded of an incident with my own daughter where I wanted her to listen more attentively to her teacher and other adults. I also wanted her to acknowledge that she was listening. As I had failed through various activities, I decided to examine my own behaviour. I asked myself the question, "How was I listening to her wishes?" By listening to her more carefully and acknowledging that I was listening to her, I was finally able to affect her behaviour. It was not accomplished at my pace or in the manner I had expected, but on her terms, following her agenda.

'I believe that the challenging behaviour of boys and their current academic underachievement is a direct result of the way we socialise them. As toddlers, boys express their emotions as much as girls and show equal interest in social games such as playing with dolls and cuddly toys. But as they mature, we tend to discourage boys from participating in games like these. Instead, we offer them toy guns, cars and construction games. While these types of games develop their problem-solving skills and spatial awareness, they do not promote social interaction. In addition, because boys are not encouraged to express their feelings – other than anger and aggression – they have little outlet for them other than through their behaviour. It's a prime example of the self-fulfilling prophecy in action.

'There are many changes I'd like to see for the future of education. I'd like to see education becoming a more fulfilling and exciting adventure for teachers, parents and children. Teaching needs to be more about modelling behaviours and the creation of a learning-by-discovery mode. I'd like to see the creation of learning environments that cater for children of varied learning styles and abilities. Schools need to pay more respect to the individuality of each child and place greater emphasis on creativity. There also needs to be greater cooperation between parents and teachers, as well as an awareness and desire from both parties to take more responsibility for continually developing themselves, the better to model children. This can best be achieved if teachers and parents make space for their own self-reflection. I'd like to see fewer victims amongst teachers and parents and more individuals taking control of learning environments. Finally, education needs to spill over into all aspects of our lives rather than being boxed in and viewed as an unpleasant, chore-like chunk of our existence.'

Jenny Mosley has had 20 years experience as a teacher/educator, drama therapist and education consultant. She founded The Whole-School Quality Circle Time Model to help schools enhance self-esteem, encourage positive behaviour, develop respectful relationships and release excellence. She is the author of many books, a lecturer at Bristol University and the mother of three children.

'The concept of sitting in a circle and working as a team has been around for thousands of years. Among those who used it were the North American Indians, who handed a feather to anyone who had something to say; the Anglo-Saxons, who used the "moot circle" for standing together for debate; and Aboriginal tribes who handed round a pebble if someone wanted to express an opinion. Many of the things I do in Quality Circle Time are drawn from historical, traditional and cultural events including meditation, imagery, storytelling, puppetry, yoga and philosophy. All these activities are designed to embrace the spiritual, emotional, intellectual and physical elements which exist in all human beings. Industry has been using a similar method of 'quality circles' since the 1960s to overcome the gulf that can develop between management and the shop floor, leading to a 'them and us' attitude. The idea of sitting and communicating in a circle is a powerful multi-purpose tool. It encourages eye contact and the use of body language as well as linguistic and emotional responses which can be used by any age group from as young as two- to three-year-olds.

'For me, it all started when I was teaching at Clapham Junction Primary School in London. I was fortunate to have a head teacher who was committed to listening to everyone in the school – from the teachers, the children, the secretary, [to] the cook, the caretaker and the cleaners. He was the first person I'd ever met who was open to the idea of getting children and adults into circles, listening to them and allowing them to express an opinion. It was his democratic attitude that inspired me to develop Quality Circle Time from 1986 onwards.

'My model for Quality Circle Time was designed as a group listening system suited to a whole-class context, providing an emotionally safe place for pupils to explore what they think and feel. It was not designed to be a counselling forum nor a place for disclosures. It was developed as a strategy for encouraging honest communication and positive relationships, self-discipline, conflict resolution and assertive communication, alongside nurturing listening and speaking skills and cooperation.

'Emotional safety is essential whenever people are being asked to look at any aspect of self. A personality under threat becomes rigid and inflexible. It is only when we feel emotionally safe that we feel free to risk trying out new behaviours. Quality Circle Time is safe because it follows a clear structure of ground rules with the group, moving from "warm-up" exercises and fun, which are designed to help break down the tensions between individuals, into "a round", where everyone is given the opportunity to speak individually. This activity offers individuals a few minutes to be the centre of attention as the whole group is listening intently. It can be a very powerful tool for raising self-esteem. The round progresses to "open forum", where issues and individual problems are aired and brainstormed. This is followed by an activity which often leads to an individual or group action plan. The group is then given an opportunity for "celebration", where the pupils are encouraged to thank group members for their contribution to the group dynamics, before it finally moves to "closure", which might encompass some form of reflection or visualisation.

'It is a system based on respect, valuing and reflecting back to participants a positive mirror of their true selves. No one may put anyone down; no name may be used negatively, which protects parents, pupils, teaching and non-teaching staff from the possibility of exposure to ridicule; only one person speaks; everyone must listen; everyone has a turn and a chance to speak but anyone can choose to pass; and the teacher/facilitator has to model positive, warm and respectful behaviour. A whole-school policy that embraces the use of circle time ensures that spiritual, moral, social and cultural development are not left to chance and are at the heart of the school.

'My "circle time for adults", sessions offer the whole school staff opportunities to work on maintaining emotional safety and to work on specific relationship skills such as taking a genuine interest in others by listening well to whoever is speaking, respecting people's rights to hold an opinion, to avoid making judgements, to stay calm and non-defensive, to be prepared to sometimes apologise and forgive often. It has the potential to help teachers reconnect with their original respect for children. In recent years, many teachers have come to feel that their main task is to push children through academic hoops. Many have lost that sense of relationship with the children that originally drew them into teaching. They need to be reconnected with whatever it was that made them become a teacher. It is essential that they are heard and supported if they are to give to children.

'I believe many children's behavioural problems stem from not knowing how to play with each other. Break times and lunchtimes can be experiences of fear, loneliness and boredom. Feelings of being left out or picked on can be engendered and exacerbated. Those who supervise the breaks can feel beleaguered in the face of noisy, aggressive or frustrated children. It's important to create possibilities for all kids to join in a range of activities, to find ways of relating to each other in caring and inclusive ways. It also means providing quiet places for them to go to, such as meditation areas, which might include a water feature as well as areas for action and play.

'The Quality Circle Time Model recommends that schools teach playground games and "zone" the playground into activity areas that can be supervised by older children who have been appointed as playground patrols. Other strategies include the formation of a community service-type task force for all children who want to be constructively occupied and football parliaments to ensure that football contributes to the positive ethos of a school and not against it. We recommend that lunchtime supervisors are given the same rights as teachers and use the same incentive and sanction system whilst also being invited to regular circle time meetings with children and other members of staff.

'In my experience, when schools fail to develop a lunchtime policy, children will learn that moral values are only practised inside buildings of power. Outside in the playground, they see their own needs and those of their peers being ignored while they are left to survive in any way they can, in an emotionally barren wilderness.'

Extracts from the song
'Nothing to Declare'
by Felicity Buirski

We inoculate our children
With the virus of our fear
And make sure to top it up
With every passing year
We make them feel alone
At school and at home...

We monitor their progress
With unhealthy competition
Create jealousy and hatred
And children of perdition
Keep them in splendid isolation
Where there's no contamination
So the family can survive –
Though more dead than alive...

Divide and rule
At home and at school
Calling one child wise
Calls his brother a fool...
One we can despise
And the other one adore
Polarised projections
Of the self we love and hate
Can we heal the split inside our souls
Before it's all too late?

Useful Organisations

Alite (Accelerated Learning in Training and Education) Ltd., Bourne Park, Cores End Road, Bourne End, Bucks SL8 5AS. Tel: 01628-810700, e.mail: office@alite.co.uk, website: www.alite.co.uk

Antidote ('The organisation that promotes emotional literacy'), 3rd Floor, Cityside House, 40 Adler Street, London, E1 1EE. Tel: 0207-247-3355, e.mail: emotional.literacy@antidote.org.uk, website: www.antidote.org.uk

ChildLine, 45 Folgate Street, London, E1 6GL. Tel: 0207-650-3200, Children's Helpline 0800-1111, e-mail: supportservices@childline.org.uk, website: www.childline.org.uk

Gingerbread (Lone-Parent Families), 7 Sovereign Close, Sovereign Court, London, E1W 3HW. Tel: 0207-488-9300, e.mail: Ginger@gingerbread.demon.co.uk, website: www.gingerbread@org.uk

Jenny Mosley Consultancies, 28a Gloucester Road, Trowbridge, Wiltshire BA14 0AA, Tel: 01225-767157, email: circletime@jennymosley.co.uk, website: www.circle-time.co.uk

Kidscape, 2 Grosvenor Gardens, London, SW1W 0DH. Tel: 0207-730-3300, e-mail: info@kidscape.org.uk, website: www.kidscape.org.uk

Montessori Education (UK), 21 Vineyard Hill, London SW19 7JL. Tel: 0208-946-4433, e-mail:meuk@montessorieducationuk.

org, website: www.montessorieducation.org

Mouchel Parkman Learning Services, West Hall, Parvis Road, West Byfleet, Surrey KT14 6EZ. Tel: 01932-337000, e.mail: info@mouchelparkman.com, website: www. mouchelparkman.com

National Council for One-Parent Families, 255 Kentish Town Road, London NW5 2LX. Tel: 0207-428-5400, e-mail: info@ oneparentfamilies.org.uk, website: www.oneparentfamilies. org.uk

NSPCC, Weston House, 42 Curtain Road, London, EC2A 3NH. Tel: 0207-825-2500, 24-hour helpline for children and young people concerned about a child or young person at risk of abuse, Freephone 0808-800-5000, e-mail: help@ nspcc.org.uk, website: www.nspcc.org.uk

Parentline Plus, 520 Highgate Studios, 53–79 Highgate Road, Kentish Town, London NW5 1TL. Tel: 0207-284-5500, 24-hour Free Confidential Helpline 0808-800-2222, e-mail: centraloffice@parentlineplus.org.uk, website: www. parentlineplus.org.uk

Relate (relationship counselling), Herbert Gray College, Little Church Street, Rugby, CV21 3AP. Tel: 0845-456-1310, e-mail: enquiries@relate.org.uk, website: www.relate. org.uk

Re:membering Education, 66 Beaconsfield Villas, Brighton, E. Sussex, BN1 6HE. Tel: 01273-231367, e-mail: remember@ mcmail.com, website: www.remember.mcmail.com

Samaritans, The Upper Mill, Kingston Road, Ewell, Surrey KT17 2AF. Tel: 0208-394-8300, 24-hour helpline: 08457-909090, e-mail: admin@samaritans.org, website: www.samaritans.org

Steiner Waldorf Schools Fellowship, Kidbrooke Park, Forest Row, East Sussex, RH18 5JA. Tel: 01342-822115, e.mail: info@swsf.org.uk, website: www.steinerwaldorf.org.uk

Teacher Support Network, Hamilton House, Mabledon Place, London WC1H 9BE. Tel: 0207-554-5200, Teacher Support

Line: 0800-0562-561, e-mail: enquiries@teachersupport.
info, website: www.teachersupport.info

Young Minds (a children's mental health charity), 102–108
Clerkenwell Road, London EC1M 5SA. Tel: 0207-336-
8445, Parents' Information Service Helpline: 0800-018-
2138, email: info@youngminds.org.uk

Index

201

205

207

208

209

210

211